ReAwakening

AN ACCIDENTAL LIFE

book one

BONNIE THOMLEY

This is a work of fiction. Characters, names, and events are products of the author's imagination or are used fictitiously. Any similarity to actual persons, living or dead, is coincidental and not intended by the author.

www.bonniethomley.com

This book is dedicated to my mom: A beautiful soul with a big heart and an even bigger sense of humor. Thank you for always believing in me. I wish you were here to see this.

PROLOGUE

"What are you doing here, James? What the hell is going on?"

"There's no time to talk about this now. Run, Amy! Just run like hell! Get out of here!"

I did what he said and started running through the woods as fast as I could. It was so dark. Visibility was just impossible. The trees breezed by me as I raced toward the river. Twigs and small branches were slapping me in the face with each step that I took. Countless thorns tore through the flesh on my ankles with every step. The adrenaline pumping through my veins was so intense that I didn't even notice the pain. I could hear explosions going off behind me. Explosions booming so loudly that I could barely hear the sound of my racing heartbeat. The smell of smoke consumed the entire area so much that I could barely breathe without coughing. I tried to block out the screams of my cohorts howling in the night, but it was no use. Their cries for help filled the air. I thought about turning back so many times, but I just kept running. Maybe someone nearby would call for help. No, this place was too isolated for anyone to hear what was happening. The nearest homes and businesses were at least 20 miles away. The river was never traveled. It was too difficult to get to. Most people usually turned back before they made it even close to the water. There were no roads or bike trails in sight. Not a single place for anyone to be. It was the middle of nowhere. I feared that this gruesome attack would fall silent in the night. I wanted to turn around. I wanted to run back to find survivors, but I knew it was too late. If there was anyone left alive, they wouldn't be that way for long.

I had to keep running. It was the only thing that I could do to save myself.

I didn't have time to think about the obliteration that was fading behind me. I pushed it all out of my mind as I continued to race toward the riverbank. I knew that if I could just make it to the water, the current would carry me to safety. If I could manage to stay afloat long enough, that is. The river would eventually lead me out to the town's main road. From there I hoped to be able to walk to safety. I could not go home to my apartment, though, for someone would surely be waiting for me there. If anyone knew that I had made it out of the warehouse alive, they wouldn't sleep until I was dead like everyone else.

Thankfully I had mapped out an escape route out several weeks ago. Everyone thought that I was being overly paranoid at the time. I guess they were wrong. The truth was that even then I feared this might happen. I had always been taught to hope for the best but to prepare for the worst and that was exactly what I did. There had been a twinge in my gut that was telling me something wasn't right, but I went along with the plans anyway. Until now, I had no idea just how right my suspicions were. Had someone betrayed us? I couldn't think of anyone that would do that. Everyone that knew about what would be going on at the warehouse was now dying inside of it. There had to be some other explanation.

I was almost at the water now; I could hear it crashing against the makeshift dock that was half rotted away. When I spotted it, I knew it would be a good entry point to the river. It was so broken down that it would go unnoticed. Nobody would be stopping on their river journey to dock there. It was safe. Just a few more yards to go and I could make my getaway.

And then, all I could see was his face. James… He told me to run away. That was just like him trying to save me before he thought about fending for himself. I knew he wouldn't have let me stay to help him even if I had tried, but I was still guilt-ridden for leaving my brother behind. Would he make it out alive? Or would he be just another body left smoldering in that warehouse? But why the hell was he even there in the first place? I never told him about the research I was doing. There was no logical reason for James to know that anything was happening there today. Or ever happening there, for that matter. I hadn't spoken to him in almost a year. How did he know where to find me? The only way he could be involved in any of this would be if he was the enemy. I couldn't let myself think about that now. I had to hope that he would find a way to stay alive. I promised myself that he would come out of this unscathed and I would be able to interrogate him about all of this in the coming weeks.

I finally made it to the dock where I had a makeshift raft waiting. I pulled it from the trees that I had concealed it in when I was mapping out the area. I pulled the camouflage blanket off of it and jumped into the water. Just as I had hoped, the current was strong today. It quickly began to whisk me away from the personal hell I had just been in. As I lay back in the raft, I began to think about all of those left behind. They had been my friends, my allies, and my brother. I wondered if it had all been in vain. All of the months I spent consumed with research and lurking around dark alleys… all of the sweat and tears it took to plan this day out. Now, in the blink of an eye, it was all gone. Every shred of evidence, every witness, had just been incinerated. As I tried to blink back the tears I could feel forming, I saw the clearing that would lead me to the road into town. I began to feel a sliver of hope...a glimmer of faith assuring me that perhaps I would be the victor after all.

To my advantage, there were no people around the road. I could only imagine how I looked right now. My clothes were tattered, my skin wet and dirty, trails of tears left on my burning cheeks. If anyone was to see me right now, surely they would be suspicious of something. I would be skeptical if I saw someone in the state that I was currently in. The cops would be called in a heartbeat. That was something I did not need right now. I did my best to stick to the tree line, out of the way of any cars that were on the road this time of night. I wandered down the road for miles before I decided where to go. My initial instinct would normally be to go to the police department, but I doubted that anyone in this small town could help me now. I could even be a suspect at this point. I was the only one left alive. I decided, instead, to find the one person that I knew would still be alive. I just had to figure out where he would be hiding.

And just as I was about to sneak into a more populated area, I woke up in a sweat. What a crazy dream.

CHAPTER ONE

"Good morning, beautiful." Alex smiled as the sun hit my face. I scrunched up my nose and buried my face in the goose feather pillow. It was cool and refreshing on my face.

I always loved it when he greeted me that way. Even when my long hair looked like a bird was nesting in it and his t-shirt consumed my petite frame, he still had the ability to make me feel like a beauty queen. Today though, that wasn't the case. All I wanted to do right now was cry myself back to sleep.

"It can't be morning yet… I'm not ready to face today. Can't we just go back to sleep? Let's just lay here together until tomorrow gets here." I moaned as I rolled over. I pulled the covers over my head and laid silently. I knew I was being over dramatic, but I didn't care. I didn't want to get out of bed. I wished that I could close my eyes and wake up the next day. I didn't want to deal with any of the memories and emotions that this day would surely bring back to me.

Today marked the second anniversary of my father's death and it was still something that I had no idea how to deal with. I had my good days and even more bad days. I did my best to maintain throughout the day, but no one knew how often I disappeared to go in the bathroom and cry. Not even Alex. No matter what I did, I still felt the gaping hole that had been left torn into my heart. As far as I knew, it was the same story for my mom and brother. They were there for each other, but they rarely spoke about this anymore. It was still too painful for either of them to bear. Talking about it wasn't helpful therapy for anyone. I don't care what the experts say.

The controversy surrounding my dad's unexpected demise still felt like a whirlwind to me. Dr. Thomas Brown was once a prominent scientist, at the top of his game. And as if that weren't impressive enough, he was an all-star father and husband. He rarely missed a family dinner or a game of catch in the backyard. Every recital I had, every heartbreak… he was there. He was my entire world. Then one day, he just vanished. There was no trace of him anywhere. It was as if he had been wiped off the face of the earth and the only remaining pieces of him were the memories held by those that he left behind.

Every scientist remotely near the Tennessee area had been questioned by detectives, along with every friend and family member that he had. He was loved by everyone who knew him. He had no enemies to speak of. The police had no leads… no clue as to why or where he disappeared to. It was a complete mystery to everyone.

I can still remember the first day he was gone like it happened yesterday. I awoke to a phone call from my mother, and she was completely frantic.

"I don't know what to do, Amy! Your father didn't come home from work this morning. His cell phone goes straight to voicemail and the people at his office say that they haven't seen him since he left work yesterday morning!" my mother sobbed into the phone. "Where could he be?"

"Mom, you need to calm down. I'm sure there is a reasonable explanation for this. Have you called the local hospitals?" I somehow managed to get out while fighting hard to not start crying along with her. My mind was racing but I knew I needed to be strong for her.

"Yes. None of them have admitted anyone by his name. I called the police department, but they told me I have to wait 48 more hours before I can file a missing person report. It's not unusual for him to stay at the office overnight, so I didn't think anything of it until he still wasn't here when I woke up. I am just hysterical right now! Amy please, I don't want to be by myself!" Her voice cracked and my heart hurt for how helpless she was. I'd never heard her this broken.

"I will be at your house in ten minutes. We will find him, mom. I promise."

As I hung up the phone, panic rushed through me. I had dreamt about this very thing two weeks ago. I should've said something to someone about it. Did I somehow cause this? I have always believed that many of my dreams are a glimpse into my future, but this? I've never told anybody about this belief. It sounded so crazy. Who would believe me anyway? Under different circumstances, I would think someone was crazy if they told me that. Unfortunately, I had never been able to distinguish which dreams were going to come true and which were merely dreams. It's always a toss-up. That ability would really have come in handy.

I started running through my house, trying to get

ready to head to my parent's house. I rifled through my drawers for clothes to throw on and quickly brushed my teeth. I was out of my house within five minutes still looking like I took a ride on the hot mess express. I arrived to find my mom in a disastrous condition. She was a complete wreck. Who could blame her? Once I was finally able to pull her together, we got in my car and began searching for my father.

Mom and I drove around for hours. We went up and down every street we could find and checked every establishment he had ever been to. We knocked on every door of every friend he had and checked in every bar, restaurant, and bookstore he ever did business in. We found nothing. Absolutely *nothing*.

After 48 hours had passed, my dad still hadn't been found. We called the authorities and filed a missing person report. The police conducted a massive search, along with friends and community volunteers. Everyone searched for five days straight and we still came up with nothing. There had been no clues uncovered. No trace of him was found *anywhere*. Days and weeks passed by and there had still been no added information. It was as if he had just vanished into thin air.

My once close-knit family fell apart. We all ended up alienating each other. Each person was so filled with despair that we were unable to bear even the sight of each other. The slightest glimpse of everyone sparked various memories of my father for the others. They were memories that none of us wanted to deal with. Yet the worst part was the unknown. We were unable to be hopeful that he was alive somewhere, but still unable to fully mourn our loss. How *could* we bring ourselves to mourn? We didn't even know if he was dead or alive! There was always a slim chance, we tried to keep thinking, that he would either be found or return home to us.

Months had passed when the cops finally got a call from a woman who found a body while walking her dog on a nature trail. Just as everyone feared, it was my dad. His decaying corpse was found in several segments, scattered around in a wooded area in the northeastern side of Tennessee. Everyone was shocked not only because he was dead, but because his body was almost 300 miles away from home. How could he have gotten that far and why? What was happening? No one spoke a word, but I knew we were all thinking the same thing. Why would someone murder my father and in such a gruesome way? Who would do something so hateful?

He had been the most caring, intelligent, and driven man that I had ever known. Everyone he met instantly fell in love with him. People seemed to gravitate to him and his blinding smile. He had won numerous awards, but even the scientists he bested never seemed to hold even the slightest grudge against him. They always seemed genuinely happy for his accomplishments. So why would someone want him dead?

Everyone was still reeling with despair when what was left of him was finally released to my family. My mother, Joan, arranged the funeral services. In the meantime, my brother, James, helped tie up all of my father's loose ends. I took it upon myself to go through my dad's belongings. A few things I kept for myself, but most of it I either threw away or donated to charity. I knew this task would surely be too daunting for my newly widowed mother to have to take on. She shouldn't have to be the one to do it anyway. Unfortunately, I did not get much support with what I thought was a good idea.

"Shouldn't you keep some of these things? It is like you are just throwing away our father's legacy!" James demanded when he found out what I had tasked myself with.

"What is the point, James? Dad isn't here to read his notes; he won't need to wear his clothes. Hell, he can't even give mom another hug! This isn't a burden she should have to bear." I cried out, angry that he was insinuating that I was just throwing my father's memories away. He of all people should know I wouldn't take this decision lightly.

"Amy, you are probably right, but it still seems like we shouldn't rush into clearing out anything related to dad. He was killed. It isn't like he wanted to leave us in this situation. There isn't some scandal to rid ourselves of. Do what you need to do, though. I agree that this isn't something that mom should have to deal with. I just think that you should wait."

Within a week, what was once my parent's home was just my mother's house now. Family pictures were one of the few reminders of him that remained. I even moved things around so that my mom could stay in one of the spare bedrooms. Surely, she wouldn't be sleeping in the bed she shared with dad. That would be too hard for her to do. She would never admit it, but I knew that she had been sleeping on the couch ever since his disappearance. She tried to hide it, but I could tell. I didn't bring it up though. Everyone grieves differently.

The funeral came and went, and my family was finally beginning to reconnect. Our sadness had started to fade somewhat and we were even able to laugh again. Sunday nights turned into the family night at my mom's house and the three of us never missed it. We made a strong effort to stick together… to not let our bond slip away, especially for our mother's sake. It's what dad would have wanted us to do. Had it not been for my mom, James and I would probably have slowly drifted away from each other.

We would have surely lost track of each other's lives, only stopping to call one another on holidays and the occasional birthday. Thankfully, mom made sure to remind us of who we were and how much we loved each other. She did all she could to hold on to what she had left.

And then, I met Alex.

Alex Cardwell was in his late twenties. He had a nice car, an amazing house, and looked like he should be in a sexy firefighter calendar. He had very little family, no brothers or sisters, and his parents lived on the other side of the country. This was one of the first things that appealed to me. The fact that he did not have a close relationship with his dad meant that I would not have to constantly have to think about my now non-existent relationship with my own father. Sensing that it was a dangerous topic, Alex never forced me to talk about it either. I was so very thankful for that. I know many people think that "talking things out" helps somehow, but I was definitely not one of those people. I am more at the opposite end of the spectrum. Just bottle it up and let it go. Push it down far enough that it never finds a way back up. It worked for me.

I met Alex while I was drafting an article for the local newspaper about a radical group that he was part of. As a journalist, I met a lot of people like him. They mainly protested scientific progress that they deemed "unnatural". This included stem cell research, black hole theories… that sort of thing. They were a nonviolent group that heavily relied on press coverage to convey their message. This was the picture of the kind of man my father would *never* have wanted me to be with. "Typical right-wing nut job" he would probably say, but I didn't care. Everyone has a right to their own opinion. Their agenda wasn't wrong, either. They had plenty of research to back them up. It wasn't easy though. Those with opposing views never stopped trying to discredit and shut them down. Regardless, he made me forget about my worries and that was all that mattered.

Alex had begun to fill a void that I had since the passing of my father, and it felt so good. He loved me and I worshipped the ground he walked on. He pulled me away from the black abyss that my life had become, and I would forever be grateful to him for that. Alex was truly my knight in shining armor.

However, no matter how much easier life became, I still kept thinking about something that I came across while cleaning out my father's office that day. It was a small, tattered notebook. Inside I found odd documentations and what seemed to be frantic scrawling. It made no sense to me, and I had never heard my father mention anything of the sort. **That** notebook was one of the few things that I had kept for myself. I didn't tell my mom or James about it.

This was just for me. I simply stuck it in my purse and toted it back to my house. I was always so amazed at the inner workings of my father's brain. This notebook that was full of his thoughts (even though I didn't understand most of them) was truly a gem. It was something to be cherished.

I sat down in my living room one night when I was alone and retrieved the notebook. I scanned through it page after page, trying to somehow reconnect with my dad. If I couldn't talk to him, maybe reading his thoughts and notes could make me feel close to him once again. I couldn't make heads or tails of what he had written, but there were two constants I couldn't ignore: a man by the name of Xavier Holland and something about immortality.

Immortality?

CHAPTER TWO

I needed answers and I knew that if anyone could give them to me, Alex could. He'd had to find a lot of dirt on many scientists throughout his career. If there was a scandal to be found, surely Alex would know about it. It was the first thing I brought up when I saw him again.

"Alex, have you ever heard of someone by the name of Xavier Holland?" I asked, eager for what I would find out.

Alex paused for an extremely long time before replying. "Yes… I have." He grimaced after the words left his mouth. "Xavier is the head of Nectar Corp. He is one of the evilest, most devious men I have ever come across in this business. He doesn't think twice about sacrificing someone in the name of science, but he knows the laws so well that he *always* gets away with it. I have seen many good people die at his hand. Yet time and time again he goes unpunished. Why do you ask? Where did you hear about him? He isn't someone I would expect you to know."

I could sense he was trying to hide the anger in his reply, and I didn't want to push my luck. I knew how personally Alex took this sort of thing. His passion is what fueled the fire for his protest group. It was the biggest part of his life. Many people thought that he was anti-scientific progress, but he was actually just pro-quality of life. He agreed that most scientific advances were good, but not when they hurt or jeopardized other people's lives. He did not believe that it was for the greater good if it meant the sacrifice of humanity in any way. He thought that there was always a way to preserve life without forfeiting progress. If you listened to the media, you would think he was a quack from some religious cult. That was so far from the truth.

I was uncertain whether or not to press him about this, but I *needed* to know. I had to find out who this man was and what connection he could have had to my father. This was my only chance. I would always wonder about it.

"What kind of science is he involved in?" I pressed on, hoping he wouldn't notice my failure to tell him where I heard Xavier's name.

"A little bit of everything, as far as I can tell. My group has had sources tell us stories about everything from stem cell research to pursuing… darker scientific theories."

"What do you mean by darker scientific theories?" I tried not to laugh at the way he said it. I knew it wasn't a joke to him.

"You know black holes, atom-splitting, cloning, and things of that nature."

"Have you ever heard anything about him dealing with anything related to immortality?"

"Immortality? What like vampires?" Alex laughed out loud, making me feel a little dumb.

"I… I don't know. I was just thinking out loud. Just ignore me! I'm super tired… I think I'm becoming delirious!" I tried to laugh it off, but he had to notice how uncomfortable I had suddenly become. I must sound insane. I mean, immortality? I felt like was in a science fiction movie.

What *was* I saying anyway? Did I think that my dad's death was somehow related to Xavier Holland

and… immortality? Just hearing the idea in my head sounded crazy! What exactly was immortality, anyway? Sure, I had seen the movies about it. They were mainly about vampires and Transylvania. Those were all fiction stories made up to sell movie tickets. It wasn't real. I surely didn't believe in any of that nonsense. Surely people aren't actually walking around until the end of time after being bit by a bat.

So why was I so preoccupied with this new theory that I had discovered? Maybe it was just because I was desperate to find a reason for my dad's death. Maybe I just needed some closure… we all did. This could be the way to make that happen. Or maybe it was because I felt a throbbing twinge in the pit of my stomach every time that I thought about what I read in that notebook. I couldn't shake the feeling that the pain I felt was intuition of some kind.

Maybe what I told Alex was correct; maybe I *was* just tired and delirious. I decided to sleep on it. I grabbed Alex by the hand and led him to the bedroom. We both climbed into bed and just laid there. I loved the way I felt in his arms. So warm, so safe, like nothing could get to me here. With all of these crazy emotions and thoughts surging through me, all I wanted was to be with him and forget about everything else.

I could not wait to drift off to sleep and temporarily be freed of this burden. As soon as Alex turned off the lamp, we kissed and said our goodnights. I could feel myself slowly slipping away with my head on his chest This was my favorite way to sleep. Thankfully, this mess did not follow me into my subconscious. I had dreams about a happier time when I was surrounded by family and friends. There were no worries in the world and I was free to do whatever made me happy. If only I could just stay in this dreamland forever.

When I awoke the next morning, I was being held tightly in Alex's arms. I couldn't help but smile. I loved when he stayed here with me. Lately, the nighttime had been so lonely, especially when he stayed at his own home instead of mine. I hated to be alone with nothing more than my thoughts to occupy me, particularly now that they seemed to be taking a rather insane turn. When he was here, my mind was occupied with nothing but him. I liked it that way; it kept me calm and happy. However, it was beginning to get harder to block the other thoughts out. I knew the only way to make it better was to ask Alex for help. Was it the best decision? Who knows. I hated to do this, but I felt as if I had no other choice.

"I need to talk to you about something." I slowly sat up in bed, preparing myself for what I was about to say… worried about what his responses would be.

Alex's expression appeared to be a mix between concern and apprehension. He must have known what was coming. "You can talk to me about anything, babe" he replied with hesitation in his voice. It was now or never.

"When I was cleaning out my father's things after he died, I found a notebook. I took it home with me… sort of a memento I could hold on to. When I read it, I saw crazy things, many of them written about Xavier Holland."

"So *that* is why you asked me about him yesterday."

"Yes, it is." I tried to study his expression, but there was nothing to see. He was calm.

"Well, what kinds of things did you read about?"

"I don't know. It was so hard to make out. A majority of the things he had written were jumbled together and made no sense. I don't think another scientist could even figure it out. There was one thing, though, that was mentioned many times."

"Ok, what thing was that?"

"Immortality." My hands were trembling.

Alex sat in bed very quietly. I immediately felt regret for telling him what I just had. I began to panic. "Did I say too much? Why is he so quiet?" I kept thinking to myself. My mind was racing. Just as I was about to scramble to find something to say, Alex spoke up.

"About two years ago, I started hearing rumors that Xavier was experimenting with something he called 'immortality serum.' Nobody knew what was in it, or exactly what it could do. He injected several people with the concoction, and they died. No charges were brought against him because they were all willing participants. He was paying them for their service, and they had even signed release forms. Who would sign a release form agreeing to have some mad man make you immortal? The craziest part was that these people were his former employees! The rumor is that once he finds a formula that works, he plans to inject himself with it. He thinks that it would give him undeniable power."

"Oh my God. How could my dad possibly have been connected in this? Did you ever hear anything about the two of them being associated?"

"I don't know. I never heard your dad mentioned while any of this was going on. I would definitely remember that. It wasn't until the word of your dad's death spread that his name started coming up. The talk about the experiments and testing slowly faded away. It was as if something about his passing somehow affected Xavier or his research. I don't know in what capacity that is true, though. It is more like my own personal opinion. It could be completely coincidental. I tried hard to find out what that connection could possibly be, but I had no luck. My instincts told me that it really wasn't over, though. If he was that thirsty for immortal power then, I'm sure he is now. It only makes sense. That power-hungry mentality doesn't just go away."

"Wow. I don't what to say. This is all so confusing. I have to find a way to find out how this is all connected. It is the only way I will be able to make peace with my father's death."

"How are you going to do that? Amy, I worked at this for years and could never come up with anything." Trust me, I have tried *everything*.

"I don't know yet, but I have to figure something out. Maybe I could uncover something you couldn't. After all, I know my dad and you don't." I sounded so confident, but it was all a façade.

"I suppose that is true to some extent. Please, be careful Amy. Don't do anything rash. These are dangerous people. Be wary of where you dig. You might not like what you find."

"Don't worry, I won't rush into anything."

I got out of bed and headed to the bathroom to take a shower. It was as if a weight had been lifted off of me. I had been keeping this secret inside of me for two years now. It had become a burden I had to bear alone. I had been too ashamed and frightened to tell anyone about it before today. Who would have believed me anyway? To anyone else, I would have just been some girl whose grief had turned her into a lunatic.

I felt a strange combination of ease and determination now that my secret was out in the open. I had no idea what to do or where to start, but I finally felt hope that I could get to the bottom of things. It wouldn't be an easy thing to do, and it looked as if I had some long days ahead of me. This was something that had to be done.

The shower was so relaxing, and my mind was clear for the first time in a *very long* time. I shampooed my hair, shaved my legs, and just stood there soaking up every drop of hot water. I wanted to savor each second of this new semi-peaceful feeling I had. I turned off the water and dried myself off. I slid open the shower curtain and saw Alex standing there, just smiling. I smiled back at him and pulled him into the towel with me. I loved him so much and he was making my life so much easier. What would I have done without him? His support was the only thing that had been getting me through all of my issues lately. I hugged him and told him to have a good day at work. I would miss him, but I was glad that I would have time to myself today. I was surely going to be preoccupied with coming up with some sort of action plan.

I had no idea what I was going to do, but one thing was certain… I would avenge my father.

CHAPTER THREE

"I think I figured it out!" I said, almost bursting with excitement and scaring Alex a bit. I had been racking my brain for days trying to come up with a solution for my problem.

"Figured what out?" Alex responded, somewhat confused.

"I figured out how to get some answers about my dad."

"Ok, lay it on me."

"I think I can use my journalism skills to my advantage. I was hoping to somehow get some sort of PR-type job with Xavier Holland's company. All I need is a way in, and I think this would be the best way. I could easily find some answers if I were working from the inside, don't you think? You know, casually chat with people, and keep my eyes peeled."

"Amy, I don't think that is a very good idea. I told you, the man is pure evil. This idea is so dangerous."

"That is exactly why I think it is a good idea! I can't convince myself that there is an answer about my dad's death that *doesn't* involve this man. This is the perfect way to find out… working on the inside."

"No offense, but what makes you think you can even get this kind of job? It's unheard of! I can't think of a science corporation that would ever hire a PR agent just because they popped in one day and said that they wanted the job. Especially one who is a journalist fresh out of college. This is kind of absurd, Amy!" He said no offense, but his condescending tone was very offensive.

"I don't see how it is *absurd*, Alex!" I was furious not only because of the accusation that I was being ridiculous but also because he seemed to have no faith in me. "Just think about it! What power-seeking scientist wouldn't want great press for a low price? It would be an easy decision on his part. Besides, a lot of companies think having a fresh mind just out of college is a good thing. You know, being able to think outside of the box and bringing in innovative ideas? Plus, by the way you talk about them, they could use some good press."

Alex sat in silent contemplation for a few minutes.

"Look Amy, I am going to be perfectly honest with you. I just can't sit around and be a part of this, if it is what you decide to do."

I was completely taken back by the attitude I could sense in his voice now. "Why not? What are you saying, Alex?"

"What I am saying is…" he took a deep breath. I braced myself for what was certain to be a snarky comment based on the tone he had been using, but he just sighed. "Well, I'm saying that it's over between us if you make this decision." Alex slumped down in the chair he was sitting in. His head was now in his hands.

My heart started racing. I felt like I had just been hit with a ton of bricks. I had no idea why he would have to leave me for pursuing an avenue that could give me some answers. How selfish could he be?

"I don't understand, Alex. Why will you have to *leave* me if I chose to do this? Don't you see how much this could help me? How much it could help my family? Don't you care? You know how important my dad was to me. I need to know what happened to him!"

It was hard to get my words out between the tears. There was an abrupt pause after every two words as I struggled to catch my breath.

"I know that there is a chance it could help. Trust me, I know this, and I think it is great that you are fighting to find answers. I just don't feel like I can watch you spend a week discrediting everything my group has worked so hard to do. We have busted our asses, lost relationships, even lost our possessions to show the world who this man really is! For me to stay here while you try to paint a different picture for everyone would be like a giant slap in the face. It would be like I have done this all for nothing and I am afraid that all I will do is resent you for it. I *love* you, Amy, but surely you can see where I am coming from."

I sat silently on my sofa for what seemed like hours, but I am sure it was only a few minutes. I had just been blindsided. The entire time that I was coming up with this arrangement, I had banked on having Alex's support. I felt confident about everything because I thought that he would be by my side. Could I go on without him? I *did* understand how he felt, but this was my father I was talking about! Did he not see why this was so important to me? My father was dead, and I needed to know why!

I just felt like he was being selfish, but maybe I was too for that matter. What would he do in my position, though?

Finally, I found the courage to look him in the eyes. With hot, silent tears streaming down my face, I knew what I had to do. I loved him more than anything in the world, but I had to do what was best for my family. My mom deserved closure. We all did. I took a deep breath and said the only words that I thought were right.

"I do realize where you are coming from, but this will haunt me for the rest of my days if I don't do something. I don't want to lose you to do this, but I understand if I have to. I don't want to try to force you to stay with me, just for you to end up resenting me in the end. I love you, Alex."

"I love you too, Amy, but I have to go. I can't stick around while you do this. I'm sorry, truly."

There was nothing more that I could say. Alex slowly got out of the chair and grabbed his coat. This was not how I expected this day to be, at all. Never would I have guessed that the one person who made my life worth living would be walking out on me. He started to walk toward the door. It was killing me to watch him leave, but I knew he had to do this. What was the point in staying with me if he would just leave me in the end? He could never forgive me for undoing his years of hard work. Why did it have to be like this?

I slowly followed him to the door, choking back tears with each step that I took. He turned around and hugged me like he never had before. I was started sobbing so hard, I could barely even see. I didn't want to let go. I wanted to stay in his arms where it was safe… forever.

"If you change your mind, you know where to find me. I love you, Amy. Please be careful. I don't know what I would do if something bad happened to you."

"I love you too Alex. I am so, so sorry. Please, change your mind."

And with a tear, he was gone.

I sat alone in my apartment ugly crying. I was devastated. And once again, I felt alone in the world. My father was once my best friend and then he died, along with a part of my soul. Alex filled that sorrowful hole in my heart and now he was gone too. It was as if someone reached into my chest and tore the wound in my heart back open. The pain was more than I could bear. Why does everyone leave me?

I curled up in a ball on my couch as tears just poured from my eyes. My whole body kept shaking and my mind was in a state of panic. I felt like I was going to hyperventilate. What was I going to do? An hour ago, I was so sure of myself, so confident. Now, I was all alone and afraid. I knew I had to stay strong… for my family. But I had to give myself some time to grieve over this loss. Then I would pull it back together. I resolved to be stronger tomorrow. I had to be.

Things had not changed; I still had a plan to move forward with. I got up from the couch and headed to my bedroom. It felt so good to lay down. I buried myself under the covers and cried some more. It was definitely going to be a night that I would cry myself to sleep.

CHAPTER FOUR

I struggled to open my eyes the next morning. They were almost swollen shut. I must have cried all night, even in my sleep. My dreams were full of sorrows and regrets. It felt like I had been hit by a freight train. I didn't even have the will to get out of my bed. I told myself that I could have one more day to deal with my emotions and before I knew it a week had passed me by. It was all a blur.

The day finally came when I knew I had to get up and get over it. My head was throbbing from a week's worth of tears and my face hurt more than I thought possible. I almost didn't recognize myself in the mirror. Those puffy eyes, the red nose… I looked like an overripe tomato! I would have to work hard to make myself look presentable. I considered postponing my adventure until tomorrow but decided I couldn't wait any longer.

I forced myself across the room to the bathroom. I splashed cold water on my face and covered my eyes with ice cubes. If that didn't work, I would try the hemorrhoid cream trick next. It always made me laugh when my mom would put that on the bags under her eyes. She swore that it worked. I took some Tylenol and chugged a bottle of water. I walked like a zombie to my closet and got dressed. I finally managed to pull myself together after about an hour.

I had already flaked on my job at the newspaper this week, so I didn't even bother calling them to tell them I wouldn't be back any time soon. If I didn't manage to get hired at Xavier's company, then I would just blame this past week on unresolved father issues and beg for my job back. Luckily, my boss was pretty laid back.

With my resume in hand, I walked outside and got into my car. I set my GPS for Nectar Corp. and drove out of my neighborhood. The lab was about an hour away and I was grateful for that. I was unreasonably nervous and needed the long drive to mentally prepare for what I was going to say. There were so many thoughts racing through my mind that I needed to filter out. I was surprised that I was even able to get a meeting on such short notice. It had to be a good sign. All I had to do now was convince them that they needed my services. My nerves were unbearable. I started taking deep breaths and thinking positive thoughts.

"Be confident! Promote the hell out of yourself! Don't take no for an answer!" I kept chanting to myself over and over again. I focused on the reasons why they should hire me. I went over every question I thought they might ask me. What if someone asked about my father? I kept thinking about what I would say if they mentioned him. I still didn't know for sure what the relationship between my dad and Xavier was. It could have been nonexistent. I was unsure if I should even acknowledge a connection or not. Ignorance might just be bliss in this case.

Before I knew it, I was pulling into the parking lot of Nectar Corp. Luckily, there was a spot close to the front door. I figured that if I had to leave, running from the building for some reason, it would be a promising idea to be parked close. I had no idea what to expect, after all. This could potentially end badly for me. What if the breadcrumbs that I had stumbled upon were serious enough for Xavier to want to end my life as well? It was frightening not knowing what to expect. I gathered my resume, took a deep breath, and headed into the building, hoping for the best.

It took some effort to pull open the gigantic glass door. I hoped that no one saw me struggle to get inside. This was already getting off to a questionable start. The lobby had reflective floors and was surrounded by walls of windows. There was a small row of chairs and plaques on the wall that had been awarded for outstanding discoveries and helping the community. There was a large desk in the center of the room with a small blonde girl answering the phone. She smiled as I approached the desk.

"You must be Miss Brown, my name is Janelle. Mr. Gilchrist is expecting you. Have a seat and I will tell him you have arrived." She motioned to the row of chairs covered in brown leather.

I thanked the very upbeat girl and took a seat. There was a small table near the chairs that was covered with magazines. I thumbed through a few articles in Popular Science, trying to keep myself occupied. It felt like I had been sitting there for at least an hour before they called me back, but once I was up and walking I would have done anything to have more time.

"Right this way Miss Brown." The girl from the desk motioned for me.

I walked through a door behind the front desk and down an insanely long hallway until I was at Mr.

Gilchrist's office. I patiently waited, catching a glance around the room in the meantime. The office was covered in bookshelves that were filled with more books than I had ever seen in one room, even a library. There were two plush chairs in front of a plain wooden desk where Mr. Gilchrist was currently seated. In front of him was an oversized nameplate that simply said 'Martin Gilchrist.' No fancy title, just a name. I liked that. It certainly made me feel a little less intimidated.

"Please come in, Miss Brown." Mr. Gilchrist said as he stood to shake my hand. "Take a seat. Tell me, what brings you here today?" His smile was inviting.

"First of all, I would like to thank you for agreeing to meet with me on such short notice. And as to why I am here, honestly, I have noticed all of the bad press your company has been getting from Alex Cardwell's protest group lately. With my journalism and reporting knowledge, I believe I could help restore your community image."

"And why would you want to do this, exactly? What is in it for you?" I was a bit taken back by his wording, but I suppose everyone had some sort of motive.

"I believe in scientific progress… without it, our country would still be in the dark ages. I think that great discoveries often take small sacrifices. Mr.

Cardwell's group has turned the public opinion against this, and I think you deserve community support for what you are doing. The people of this city need to see the good that you are doing here. It is so important."

"While I appreciate your support, you must know that this is not the type of position we typically hire for. What kind of experience do you have that could help you accomplish what you say you can?"

"The truth is, I have only been a journalist for a little less than a year. I graduated at the top of my class, and I think I would bring some fresh ideas to the table. I also have some important contacts that could help me get the exposure that this company needs. I realize that you aren't looking for someone to fill this type of position, Mr. Gilchrist, but I really think that this would be a great choice for your company. I am not asking for much money, either. I'm not going to lie; this would be great for my career too. I think this would be a win-win situation."

I silently prayed that this man could not tell how nervous I was. I couldn't believe how steady my hand was. I thought for sure my hands would be shaking uncontrollably by now. Were they so sweaty it felt like my hands had been in the sink? Absolutely. But I managed to hold my composure as I continued with my interview.

"I am grateful for your honesty, Amy. Tell me, do you have any scientific experience in your background?"

Should I simply tell him "no" and go on with the questions, or should I confess to who my father was? I didn't know whether that information would hurt or help me. What the hell, I could always pretend to be ignorant to the fact that he had anything to do with these people.

"I personally have no real science experience in my background. I took a few extra courses in college at the request of my father, but that is about it. My father was a scientist, though, so I did hear and see quite a bit over the years."

"Your father wasn't Thomas Brown, was he?" There it was. The dreaded question. I shouldn't have been naive enough to think that no one would make the connection.

"Yes, he was. I never thought I would want to be involved in anything scientific. But when my dad died, something came alive inside of me. I think I finally see why he was so passionate about all of this. I would love to do what I can to make it more accepted by the general public. It would make me feel honored to do something to help keep the path for progress open. It is what my father would have wanted."

That last sentence almost made my eyes tear up. It was the truth. My dad was the most passionate man that I had ever known, and he would have hated to see anyone or anything stand in the way of science. In a way, I think that coming here to "work" could serve that purpose as well. How hadn't that crossed my mind before?

"I see. Well, I think we can afford to give you a try. It certainly couldn't do anything to hurt our image, as Alex Cardwell has already done that. Plus, you aren't asking for a very high salary. At the very worst, we let you go after a few weeks if you do not produce any results. At the absolute best, however, you clean our image up and we can keep you here permanently."

"Wow, I don't know what to say. Thank you very much, sir." I sounded genuinely astounded at what he had just told me and that's because I was. I never once dreamed that it would be this easy to get behind the scenes of this place. If anything, I thought I would get some lame line about thinking about things and the promises of a call back. Why *was* it this easy, I couldn't help but wonder. Was this a setup?

"Mr. Gilchrist," I just couldn't help myself "Do you mind if I ask why you are giving me this job? Does it have anything to do with who my father was?"

"If I am being perfectly honest with you, Miss Brown, yes it does. Your father was one of the most passionate scientists this world had seen in a very long time. He was a good man with more integrity that most people have these days. I can only hope and assume that you have the same passion and goodness in you, my dear. Now, if that is all squared away, you can start next week. *If* you can agree to all of our employment terms. We can set up an office for you and get you whatever resources you need. Be here Monday morning at 8. We will have a short staff meeting to introduce you to the team. I'm sure Xavier will want you to himself most of the day."

"Absolutely, Mr. Gilchrist." I shuddered at the thought of that. A day alone with Xavier Holland.

"Before you go, there is some paperwork that you need to fill out. Standard procedure type things and a few contracts."

"What type of contracts?"

"Just a few general contracts, nothing too elaborate. We do go a long way to protect ourselves here. We have to be sure that we know who we can trust. I will give you a few moments of privacy to look everything over. If you have any questions, please let me know."

He left me alone in his office. I almost didn't know where to begin. There must have been a dozen papers in front of me. There was a standard release agreeing to a background check, one was a drug test form and several other release forms. I started reading the contract and I couldn't believe my eyes. Was I really reading this?

'*By signing this contract, you are agreeing to give us the right to conduct any non-life-threatening experimental procedures on you in the event you are involuntarily terminated.*'

Were they serious? As I kept shuffling through the stack of papers, I found a release for a blood test, another contract agreeing to not partake in drugs (both illegal *and* prescription) or alcohol, and a contract agreeing that I would be on-call 24/7 for Nectar Corp. This all seemed so bizarre, but I figured it was all a necessary sacrifice to solve my father's murder. Hesitantly, I signed each form. These were frightening terms, but I couldn't back out now. Was I signing m life away? It certainly felt like I might be. I would have agreed to almost anything, though, if it meant getting vengeance for my dad in the end.

I had just put my pen down when Mr. Gilchrist reentered the room.

"So, do you have any questions? I know a lot of this must seem a bit out of the ordinary." He asked me with a small chuckle as he sat back down.

"Yes, it is a bit different, but I understand the need. I am sure that this keeps people from betraying the company. Though I do have one question. What type of experiments is that contract referring to exactly? As it stands, you might let me go in a few weeks if you are unhappy with my results. I want to be prepared for the risk I might be taking."

"I thought you might ask that. I promise that it sounds much worse than it really is. They are very safe procedures. It is mainly there to discourage employees from doing unfavorable things. More of a scare tactic, if you will. People with bad intentions usually don't bother showing up for their first day after they read that. Nevertheless, the procedures we have conducted on past employees have included gene typing, vaccine testing, drug trials, and new medication studies. All very safe things, I assure you. Nothing that would have any type of adverse or detrimental effect on someone's life."

That did make sense, surprisingly. It seemed like it would be a surefire way to find out who your allies were. But there were still more strange things in there that I couldn't let go of.

"Ok. I also noticed the part about prescription medications. I am not currently on any, but I was simply curious as to why it matters."

"We believe that you should treat your body as if it were a temple. Filling it with what are usually unnecessary medications goes against that belief.

Should you choose to take this job, we do have a doctor on staff that specializes in holistic and natural medicine. We rely on him to help us with any ailment we may encounter."

"I see. That does make sense."

"Well, Miss Brown, what do you think? Would you like to work with us?" I couldn't believe that I was actually about to say this, but there was no turning back. I had made it this far.

"I would like that very much and please, call me Amy."

"Very well, Amy. Welcome aboard. We will see you bright and early, Monday morning."

I left the building feeling empowered but broke down into tears by the time I made it to my car. The wave of emotions that hit me was so intense. It was more than I expected. I couldn't just sit in the parking lot and let them see me cry. After taking a deep breath to steady my breathing, I put the car in reverse, and pulled out of the parking lot. I could cry, scream, and even pull my hair out if I wanted to as soon as I was back in my own house.

Once I finally made it home, I was an absolute wreck. I was shaking and what was left of my makeup was now a giant mess. Spider eyes were the least of my worries. I looked like a clown. I was both overwhelmed and terrified. But I was also relieved. I got the best possible outcome… a job with the company that very well may be behind my father's demise. It was exactly what I had set out to do. What if Alex were right and I was leading myself right down the path that would lead to my demise? What had I gotten myself into?

CHAPTER FIVE

The sound of my alarm startled me awake early Monday morning. I hit the snooze button and quietly laid there. I wasn't going back to sleep, but I wasn't ready to get up just yet. I couldn't believe that it was time to start my new job already.

The weekend had gone by too quickly. I tried to relax, hoping that a peaceful weekend would calm my nerves. I took a long nature walk and even took a nap out by the local lake. I went to the movies with a few friends, but none of it worked. My brain and heart had still been overwhelmed by my emotions.

At least I was able to somewhat salvage my reputation at the newspaper. I told them that I had been under so much emotional stress because of my family and asked to take a leave of absence. It wasn't a complete lie. After all, that was what led me to where I was now. And truth be told, I *was* an emotional wreck. Though I was surprised that I had been able to hold on at work as long as I had. It was only a matter of time before I would have had to take some time off, even if the opportunity at Nectar Corp hadn't come along. My mental state was deteriorating. I had never felt so unstable.

Thank God I decided to get up extra early. I needed time to mentally prepare for my meeting with Xavier Holland. I didn't know what he looked like, how old he was or what kinds of questions he would be asking me. I could have searched online, but I was afraid of what I would find. I didn't want to come across anything that might make me chicken out. If he and my father were enemies, he would probably want to pick my brain to see how much I knew. Pretending to be blissfully ignorant of the whole situation would probably be the best approach. And hopefully, my rage wouldn't get in my way.

The drive to Nectar Corp was quicker than I remembered. Maybe I was just anxious to get this day over with already. Once I arrived, I didn't waste any time getting out of my car and into the building. The more time I took, the more likely I was to say screw it, turn the car around, and drive home. That wasn't an option. I had to see this through. I took one last deep breath and walked inside.

"Good morning, Miss Brown. It's good to see you again." Janelle at the front desk greeted me with a bubbly voice. I wished I was more of a morning person like her. Until my body was pumped full of coffee, I wasn't having it.

"It's a pleasure to see you too Janelle and please, call me Amy." This brought an even bigger smile to her face.

"Head on back, Amy, they are all expecting you."

I had only met Janelle once, but it was comforting to see her smiling face. Let's be honest, I was looking for comfort in just about *anything* right now. My heart was pounding as I started to walk down the hallway. I started going over motivational speeches in my head until I made it to Martin Gilchrist's office. At least I partially knew my way around this small portion of the workplace.

I gave myself one last "You can do this!" pep talk before I peeked into the office.

"Hello, Amy. You are right on time." He glanced at his watch. "I was heading to the conference room for the staff meeting. Why don't you follow me? I can show you to your office afterward."

I followed him down the hallway into the conference room. It was a large room that was taken up mostly by the oversized conference table. Very stereotypical and just what you would see on some lame tv show. Every seat was full, except for mine and Martin's.

"If I could have everyone's attention please, this is Amy Brown. She will be our new PR representative. She is here to turn this company's image around and start earning trust back from the community/ I trust everyone will make her feel at home." Martin announced. My heart was racing. Please God, don't let me black out or something.

"Welcome, Amy." said the man sitting at the head of the table. "I am Xavier Holland. It is a pleasure to have you here with us."

"Thank you. I am very happy to be here." I somehow managed to blurt out in a small, mousy voice. I was completely taken back. Xavier was nothing like I had pictured him to be. He was a very handsome man. I guessed that he was in his late-twenties, which is an astonishing age for someone in his position. I mean, I was 21 and he couldn't be much older than me. He had tousled blonde hair, striking green eyes, and an athletic built. I had imagined him to be the typical scary-looking mad scientist that you see in horror movies. He looked nothing like that at all. I quickly tore my stare away and had a seat at the table.

The meeting was relatively unexciting. Profits were up, but the press was still bad. Mainly due to my ex-boyfriend's group I imagined. It was a good thing that I was there to fix that, someone across the table said. If they only knew how much I hated having to do this. Other than that, no new discoveries had been made, but there was considerable progress to be seen.

As Xavier conducted the meeting, I felt like he was staring a hole right through me. Panic began to set in and I broke into an icy sweat. What if he was onto my plans? Had he assumed that I knew he was behind my father's death? I quickly began to fear what would come of the rest of my day. If he knew that I was aware of the situation, why would he ever let me leave this place? Dread had begun to set in.

As my imagination began to get completely carried away, I realized that he was dismissing everyone from the staff meeting. Crap. What had I missed?

"Amy, I would like you to stay behind. We have much to discuss." Xavier said.

"Of course, no problem." I hoped he couldn't hear the uncertainty in my voice, or the incredibly loud sound of my heart pounding out of my chest. It was almost all I could hear. I had to find a way to calm down.

Once everyone finally cleared the room, he asked me to come and fill the seat next to him and he began to talk.

"First of all, let me tell you how thrilled I am that you came to work for us. I have seen your articles in the newspaper, and I have always been impressed with your work. Not to mention that, well, your father was one of my favorite associates. He was and is still one of my idols. He did so much in the name of science. It was truly heartbreaking what happened to him. It was a monumental loss for the science community."

"Thank you. I did not know that you and my father knew each other."

So many emotions were running through me at this moment. It was hard to hold them all back. I was shocked that he had even brought my dad up. And I was even more surprised that he referred to him as one of his idols! Rage flew through me when he referenced his death. He had been the one that caused it, yet he had the nerve to act as if it *saddened* him. It took all I had to hold back my tears.

"I want you to know that we have already set up an office for you. Every resource we have here is at your disposal. I hope that you will feel free to come to any of us with any of your needs. Janelle at the front desk will be happy to make any phone calls or appointments that you may need."

"I appreciate that, Mr. Holland."

"Oh, please call me Xavier. We like to keep things as informal as possible around here. You will find that this is not your typical, stuffy office setting. Now, let me show you to your office."

We both stood up and began to leave the room. As we approached the doorway, he extended his hand motioning for me to leave first. He shut the door and moved past me as I hovered awkwardly by the door. I followed Xavier down a long hallway. My office was all the way at the end, near the lobby. It was a nice space and was somewhat separated from the rest of the offices. It was painted neutral colors and had a decent view. I had a huge desk and what looked to be an extremely comfortable chair. "It will be easy to make this office into a suitable work environment." I thought to myself.

"Well, Amy, what do you think?"

"It is absolutely perfect. Thank you."

"If there are any supplies you require that we do not currently have, Janelle can provide you with the company credit card. Just bring your invoice back to her and she will take care of the rest."

"Thanks. I don't think I will need much other than my laptop and a phone." And a therapist very soon I couldn't help but think after I finished my sentence.

"That sounds good. If you don't mind, I would like to show you the rest of the office and tell you a bit about what we do here. I just wanted to start by showing you your new office space."

"That would be great. I need to know everything I can if I am going to reverse the damage Alex Cardwell has done to your image." I knew I was being absurd, but just saying Alex's name almost brought tears to my eyes. This was going to be harder than I thought. In order to do my job well enough for anyone not to suspect that I was up to something else, I was going to have to discredit everything Alex had worked so hard to prove. I felt like the worst person in the world. I didn't blame Alex for leaving me over this… I would have left me too.

I followed Xavier to the elevator and was surprised to see that the building had nine levels. It looked so much smaller from the outside. There were five levels above the ground and four below.

"I will show you all of the upper levels first. They are where we do most of our pharmaceutical research. We do many drug trials and patient studies. There are private rooms for the participants. We prefer that they stay here during the trials so that they can be closely monitored."

He took me floor by floor. I saw numerous labs where they were obviously doing drug research. Next were the rooms where the patients stayed. They were remarkably similar to the private rooms that hospitals use for sleep studies, but they were also equipped with a refrigerator and a small dining area. It was a setup that people would feel comfortable enough to stay in for these trials. There was nothing out of the ordinary. I did the best I could to hide my disappointment. I was hoping that there would be something that would catch my eye. Something that I could go back to investigate later, but there was nothing of the sort.

After we finished the upper-level tour, he took me down below. I was a bit surprised when he made a call first to someone alerting them that we were on our way down. Was he trying to hide something or were they just not used to having visitors?

"Amy." He said my name in such a way that sent a chill down my spine. It was stern, yet soft, but demanded attention.

"Yes, Xavier?" I look at him, praying that he didn't see the fear in my eyes.

"Most of what goes on down here is top secret. A lot of it is controversial, cutting edge, even frowned upon by other sectors. They are envious of the advances we have made here. The general public doesn't agree with most of it, so we try to keep it quiet. What people aren't familiar with tends to frighten them. It is understandable, but still very frustrating. What you are about to see is the reason you had to agree to such extreme employment terms."

I stayed quiet and nodded, ready to keep my eyes peeled. It was hard, but I managed to dull down the surplus of thoughts that had been running rampant in my head.

We started on sublevel one. The scientists here were doing stem cell research. I thought that the government had banned this sort of thing. From the looks of it, though, the ban never existed here. They appeared to be too far advanced for there to have been an eight-year break in the study.

"We get funding from a secret government agency for our stem cell research. We had to bribe some powerful officials to be able to conduct these experiments before the ban was lifted." Xavier continued. "What lies down here you may never discuss or write about. I don't care how much it could help, it has to stay under wraps."

"I understand. Have you had much success with the research?" I replied wearily, trying to stay engaged.

"Yes, we have. We are learning which diseases

respond to it. We feel that we are very close to having the cure for several things. What a wonder it would be to free people from the burdens of things such as Parkinson's and MS."

"That *would* be amazing."

We returned to the elevator and ventured below to the next floor. Cloning... I should have easily guessed that.

"This is where we conduct our cloning studies. You don't hear much about our doing this, mainly because we do not limit our studies to animals. Because of this, we do not even speak of the discoveries we have made with the animals. We would have too many people nosing around. We would be ruined if anyone knew were trying to clone humans. And even if we do manage to successfully clone another human being, we would never share our success. Too many people look at this as a crime against God. It would never be accepted. I wouldn't put a person who has been cloned through that. Imagine what kind of outcast they would be made into. It would tear them down mentally. This breakthrough would be more of a personal victory."

"That is a very compassionate standpoint." I said, genuinely sounding surprised.

"It's the truth. This world is cruel enough to someone who doesn't have that kind of disadvantage.

I am a scientist, not a monster."

Not a monster? So many thoughts were racing through my mind right now. I *had* pictured this man as a monster, but the kindhearted side of him that I was seeing now left me feeling conflicted. I no longer knew what to think. This was more confusing than I had expected it to be.

We continued onto sub-level three. They were splitting atoms here. I had heard stories about this. People were battling on both sides of the subject. This is precisely why people were predicting the world's end in 2012.

"Atom splitting, right?" I asked, trying to sound somewhat informed. My dad would have gotten a chuckle out of that.

"That is correct." Xavier sounded surprised that I was able to identify what I was seeing. "A lot of other corporations are doing this right now. We didn't want to be left out of the fun. We aren't doing anything different than the rest of them. However, it would be rewarding to beat them to the breakthroughs."

Xavier seemed to hesitate before going to the last floor. I wondered what could be down there… and if I really wanted to know.

"Do you want to go on, or would you like to go get settled in?"

I knew that was an indication that *he* did not want to go further, but I didn't come all this way to turn back now.

"No way. I'm anxious to see what awaits us." I said excitedly, unwilling to give in to what he wanted.

"Very well. Away we go." And with that, we were in the elevator, on our way to the last stop.

The elevator stopped and we waited there for a moment before the doors opened.

"This is the most controversial and sacred part of our research efforts. When we started getting bad press from Mr. Cardwell's group, we acted as if we entirely shut down this part of the lab. Although, the truth is that this is what we have been most vigorously working on. This is my brainchild."

When the doors opened, I couldn't believe my eyes. Could this be what I thought it was? It most definitely was. The Holy Grail. This could be my key to everything.

"We are testing several different things here, looking for the same end result… immortality. What we are doing got so misconstrued. People said we were trying to create zombies and vampires. It is nothing like that at all! This is not some twisted horror movie. I don't know why people who hear about this automatically assume we are using this research for a negative purpose. Think of the positives that this could create! What if we could save people indefinitely? Say someone you knew was dying from a terminal illness… what if you could make them immortal? What if you could *save* them?"

This bewildered me even more. Xavier made this sound as if it were a *good* thing. That was impossible! It didn't make sense to me that my father could have died because of something positive…. Something good for mankind. There had to be more to the story that he wasn't mentioning. Besides, who would want to live forever anyway?

"What do you think, Amy?"

"I… I don't really know how I feel about the subject. I think it has good and bad sides to it, but I'm not sure which side I think outweighs the other."

"Yes, well I'm sure you will have plenty of time to see both sides while you are here. The only thing I ask is that you do not ever mention what you have seen here today. You must realize how detrimental that would be for us."

"Of course. Besides, I am trying to improve your image and these things would just make it more turbulent."

"My thoughts exactly. There is one more thing that we are working on down here. Not too controversial, but still top secret."

I was so intrigued! I couldn't think of anything else that would be down here. It seemed like we covered all of the taboo topics already. What could be left?

"Have you ever had a dream, so vivid, so real that you thought it was real?"

"Yes, I believe that I have." A chill ran down my spine as I thought about how much of a reality dreams are for me. I wouldn't dare tell him that, though. He would probably poke and prod me like a lab mouse just so he could figure out a way to use my experience.

"Well, that's what we are trying to do. We are working on a way to turn a dream into reality."

"That would be amazing. I mean, how many times have we all had a dream that we didn't want to wake up from?" I said, trying to sound enthusiastic.

"Exactly. The research is only in the beginning stages right now, though. We still have a long way to go. I think that the key is finding a link between dreams and raw psychic ability. It sounds far-fetched, I know, but I genuinely believe there is something real to be found."

"That is a very interesting theory. I would love to hear more about it." I couldn't believe the words were coming out of my mouth! I hated this man and all I could manage to talk about is how interested in his research I was? I had to get out of this place as soon as possible.

"Well, now that you have seen everything, why don't we return to the surface?"

"You read my mind, Xavier."

We returned to the main floor and made our way to Xavier's office. It was almost exactly how I had pictured it. The walls were obscured by bookshelves that were packed with books about zombies, vampires, paranormal activity, and every scientific topic you could think of. But there were also several pictures of Xavier with what appeared to be special needs children.

"Those pictures are of children that we offered free services to. They were all candidates for various clinical trials, so we invited them in to see if we could help." He must have seen me looking.

"Wow. That is really amazing. And I don't think I have ever seen this many books in one place other than a library. A very impressive collection you have here."

"Thank you. I'm really just a packrat when it comes to books. I can't seem to bring myself to get rid of any of them. You should see my office at home. It is even worse." He chuckled and I couldn't believe that I was standing here having this conversation.

"I appreciate the tour of the building. If you don't mind, though, I'd like to get to my office and start turning it into my second home."

"Yes, by all means. If you need anything, you know where to find me."

"I sure do. See ya later."

I turned and walked down the hallway to my office. I closed the door and sank down into my new office chair. I didn't know what to do with all of the thoughts running wild in my head right now. There was so much to process. I began the day thinking that I would spend it with a murderous villain, but now I felt like he was just a compassionate scientist instead. This would be a tougher task than I originally imagined. What was I getting myself into?

Perhaps I should just do some real work today and deal with my insane imagination later. I opened the list of contacts I had on my laptop and started placing calls. I needed to somehow run a positive article about Nectar Corp in every publication that Alex had bad-mouthed them in. Where should I even start?

Hours had passed and I was completely consumed in setting up a contact list. I wrote down the name and phone number of everyone that I thought would possibly help me publish a story about Nectar Corp. I was so engrossed in what I was doing that I almost jumped out of my seat when someone knocked on my office door.

"Come in." I called, with my nose still buried in phone numbers. I had no time to stop now. Thank God I was good at multi-tasking. I could easily continue work and talk at the same time.

"It's six o'clock, Amy. Are you leaving soon?"

I looked up from my desk to see Martin Gilchrist standing in my doorway.

"It is six o'clock already? I completely lost track of time. Is anyone else left in the building?"

"Nope, it's just us. Everyone else left a few hours ago. Only the scientists in the sublevel labs stay here at night. You can stay if you'd like, but I'd really prefer it if I didn't leave you all alone. I don't mean to be offensive... I guess I just have a protective nature."

"No offense taken, Martin. I appreciate that, actually. Give me just a moment to gather my things. You wouldn't mind walking me out, would you?"

"No, not at all. I will wait for you in the lobby. Take your time."

I closed my laptop and shoved it into my bag. I was so relieved to have made it through my first day. I certainly felt more confident about blending in here for as long as I needed to. Perhaps I would give it a few days before I began snooping for evidence. It would be best to lay low for a while, after all.

I met Martin in the lobby and we walked to the parking lot together. Thankfully, he didn't try to make a lot of small talk. I bid him goodnight as I got into my car. It was enthralling to be on my way home. I felt so mentally exhausted. I wanted nothing more than to sink into my couch and drift off to sleep. I would love a glass of wine, but I didn't want to go against that contract on my first day. God only knew what kind of experiment they would try to perform on me! I decided to go to sleep instead.

That night I dreamt of Xavier and Nectar Corp., or maybe it was a nightmare. Either way, it was all that I could think about, even subconsciously. It was as if I couldn't escape it.

I could see him smiling at me. He was coming toward me as if he were going to hug me and I was happy that it was about to happen. I wiped tears off of my cheeks and smiled back at him. All I could say was "thank you."

I had to be stronger than this and the easiest way to do that would be to forget all about this stupid dream! Dreams didn't mean anything for God's sake. How many crazy dreams had I dreamt over the years that were just that? Nothing else. Xavier was a fool to think otherwise. So was I for that matter. I would just have to take it one day at a time. The truth could be within my reach if I focused on it hard enough. I had to put in the work. After all, Xavier was still a killer… and I would still show the world who he really was.

CHAPTER SIX

Two weeks had passed since my eventful first day and I was getting settled in nicely. I had written more articles and placed more phone calls than I could remember. I had been so overwhelmed with work that I hadn't had much time to follow my main objective, which was to uncover the truth. There was a lot to show for my time, though. I had managed to have articles published about Nectar Corp in several very popular newspapers. As much as I hated shedding a positive light on this place, I had to admit that I was immensely proud of what my hard work had accomplished. I just wished that I had uncovered some sort of controversy by now.

I hoped that today would be the day for that to change. Fridays were a half-day at the office. Even Xavier usually left by noon on Friday. Today should be no different. I had purposefully been the only person that didn't leave early the past two weeks. I expected that this could work to my advantage today because no one would think my presence was out of the ordinary.

Planning for this day had taken all week. I made sure to get all of my work done in the first few days so I would have nothing holding me back. It was exhausting but necessary. I wanted my day to be completely open. I planned to pretend to be working vigorously until everyone else left and then I would spring into action.

I stayed in my office with the door shut most of the day. There had been several knocks at my door throughout the day, mostly from Martin and Xavier. They both still seemed so concerned about whether I had all of the resources that I needed or not. I thought that they would lay off by now. In just two weeks I had easily begun turning their public image around. Clearly, that should mean that I had everything that I needed. If not, their press would still be horrible. My work should speak for itself! But it did make me feel that they weren't suspecting me of having a sinister agenda. Otherwise, I wouldn't be working my ass off to save theirs, or so I assumed they thought.

I buried myself in nonsensical paperwork until staff members started to trickle out of the building. One by one they passed by my office on their way to the lobby. I kept a headcount as they went by. It was close to 12:15 and I determined that the only person left was Xavier. Should I go see what his plans were for the rest of the afternoon, or should I just sit and wait? I decided to wait it out. There was no reason to be anxious now; it would probably just blow my cover.

Just as I had made my decision, Xavier showed up at my doorway.

"Are you staying late again today, Amy?"

"It's hardly late, Xavier. It's not even 12:30 yet."

"I know, but it's Friday. You are the only one who has it in them to stay past noon. Take a break today. It's a beautiful day outside and you should be out enjoying it."

"I know I should, but I still have so much to do. If I don't finish everything today, it will haunt me all weekend. Not to mention what a pain Monday will be for me."

I hoped he didn't sense that I was just making

up excuses. God help me if he wanted to know what work I had left. I didn't know what I would say. There was absolutely nothing left for me to do. I had been doodling and making a grocery list for the last four hours.

"If you say so. If it gets too late, call security and they can walk you to your car. Have a wonderful weekend, Amy."

"Thanks, Xavier, same to you. See you on Monday."

He smiled and was gone. I breathed a long sigh of relief. Maybe it would be a good idea if I waited in my office for a while longer. There was no reason to risk getting caught just because I was impatient. What if he forgot something in his office and came back to find me snooping around? My chances would be up, not to mention they would probably try to conduct experiments on me. Surely I could manage to wait a few more moments.

Twenty minutes had passed and I figured the coast should be clear. I casually walked to the lobby. I stopped at the front desk and acted as if I were looking for something. After glancing through the windows, I saw no other cars in the parking lot. I was free to nose around. I turned back around and walked toward the offices. Where would the best place to start looking for clues be? I walked down the hallway toward Xavier's office. If there *was* anything to find, this would be the place to find it. As I got to the door, I said a quick prayer that it would be unlocked. Today was my lucky day. I twisted the door handle and walked right in.

A jolt of adrenaline ran through me as I entered the room. I quickly walked over to his desk and began neatly digging through the drawers. I started with the top drawer, but only found pens and basic office supplies. The second was equally disappointing. It contained many manila folders, but all they contained was different drug trial statistics. The third drawer was a complete mess. I had to dig through a cluster of various papers, science magazines, and more office supplies. At the very bottom of the clutter, I saw a plain black notebook. I carefully slid it out from under everything else and started thumbing through the pages. It seemed to be a mixture of thoughts, equations, and journal entries. I quickly started scanning through the pages, looking for something to catch my eye. My heart almost stopped when I saw a passage that seemed to be written about my father. It was different than the other things Xavier had written down. This was not neatly written and it all seemed to be a bit hasty. I sat down in his chair and began reading.

"I don't know whether it was a good or bad idea to involve Thomas in this whole immortality disaster. He is so hard to

read. I told him what I was doing and he was completely reactionless! It is maddening! You tell someone that you are trying to create eternal life and they say nothing. Nothing! What does that even mean? I guess there are only two possible outcomes.

Option A: He is intrigued by my research. Perhaps he will want to know more about what I am doing and how I am testing it. Maybe he would even like to offer me his scientific expertise. There could potentially be a partnership in the works. I would surely find the grouping of components with his help. What would be in it for him, though? I have no intention of going public with my discovery. There would be no fame in it, just personal and professional satisfaction.

Option B: He is revolted by what I am doing. He could do so many things that would be detrimental to my development! He could go to the government and tell them what is going on. They would shut me down in an instant! My only hope would be that perhaps someone with influence would be thirsty for more. They would certainly be able to see what kind of power immortality could bring. He could also go to the press. If the public found out what I was doing, there would be pandemonium. Sure, it was turbulent when Alex Cardwell started stirring the pot, but many did not believe him. Few would doubt an esteemed scientist like the great Thomas Brown. Religious fanatics would come at me with guns blazing. I would be lucky to even escape with my life.

So now, I am faced with a situation that I do not know how to handle. If Thomas wants to help me, then that is fantastic. If he does not, however, I cannot let him speak of this to anyone. So how do I handle this? This is a man that does not take kindly to threats. He has no apparent weaknesses other than his family. He has shown no emotion regarding anything else in his life. What will I do?"

I couldn't believe my tear-filled eyes. What had I just read? Was this a frantic plot to shut my father up? I quickly closed the notebook and put everything back just as I had found it. I left Xavier's office and ran to my own. What did I expect to find? It was destined to be something bad. I had to get out of this place immediately! I swiftly gathered my belongings and speed-walked out of the building. I opened my car door, threw in my things, and flew out of the lot. My tires squealed as I pulled onto the road. I drove as quickly as I could the whole way home. It was a miracle that I wasn't stopped by a cop. I made it to my house in what I would swear was record time.

Once inside, I locked every door and window and closed every curtain. I was scared out of my mind! What did Xavier mean by "his only weaknesses are his family"? Did that mean that my life had been in danger at one time? Was I still in danger? I curled up into a ball on my couch. I had no idea what to do. The entire time that I was planning to search for clues, I never really thought that I would actually find something that was this… direct. I imagined that I would find shreds of evidence here and there, but not a pseudo confession on paper!

I sat there on my couch for hours. There were so many thoughts running through my head, but none of them were telling me what I should do. I couldn't just ignore this, but how was I going to act around Xavier on Monday? There was no way that I would be able to act as if nothing were wrong. He just confessed to killing my father! What he wrote in that notebook showed both motive and intent. That was more than enough to convince me. But what happened? Had Xavier asked my father to help him and then murder him when he declined? Did he kill him before he had a chance to even decide? I had to find out.

How much was I willing to risk? I knew if I walked into Xavier's office Monday morning and accused him of killing my father, I would probably never make it home alive if he truly had done it. Did I have any leverage? No. Nothing that I had against him was worth anything. I had information, but he would probably just kill me before I had the opportunity to tell anyone what I knew. I could try to tell somebody before Monday. That might just give me a chance, but who would believe me? I could only think of one person... Alex. How could telling Alex keep me alive?

Hours passed as I sat and pondered how involving Alex in this could help me. He had cut me out of his life and this was exactly why. Why would he want to be intertwined in this mess now? He had told me that the only way he would ever talk to me again was if I changed my mind about working for Xavier. I was in too deep now. It was worth a shot, though, if it meant keeping myself alive. I had to try something.

I decided to write Alex a letter explaining everything that was happening at Nectar Corp. I told him about each sublevel and what they contained. I wrote down every detail about every single thing that I could remember seeing when I was down there. If Xavier tried to kill me, I would tell him about this note. I would make sure he knew that Alex would get this if I were to die. I refused to go down without a fight.

I left the note in a place where my family would easily find it while going through my things. I came up with an elaborate plan and invited my mother over for dinner Monday night. If Xavier killed me by then, my mother would notice that I was missing right away. This way, Xavier and his men wouldn't have much of a chance to go through my things before my mother was here to find them.

Xavier's only hope to keep his secrets his own would be to let me live. He would have to cooperate with me, but what did I want exactly? An explanation and a confession would be necessary, both to me and the authorities. I would agree to keep the information I knew about Nectar Corp to myself if he would turn himself in. He could turn the company over to someone else and his research could continue. I didn't care about any of that as long as my family got the closure that they deserved. I mean, I didn't disagree with most of the research that was going on anyway. Why was Alex so offended by it anyway?

I spent all weekend going over every detail of my plot. I wanted to be completely prepared on Monday. I set up the dinner plans with my mom and put the letter to Alex in the safe buried underneath the shed in my backyard. If Xavier or his men came to my house to look for evidence, they would never know to look there. The only people who knew about that safe were my family and Alex. It would be one of the first places they looked once I was missing. I also spent a good bit of time going over what I would say to Xavier. I hoped that I would be able to stay calm and rational, but I had a feeling that once I saw his smug face I was going to lose control. My heart raced at the thought of being able to avenge my father once and for all. Sunday was surely going to be a sleepless night for me.

CHAPTER SEVEN

It was no surprise that I awoke in a panic Monday morning. Today was the day that I would confront Xavier about what I found in his office. I was becoming more frightened with each passing moment. I had run so many scenarios through my head throughout the weekend. Every one of them ended up with me losing my life. It was a chance I was willing to take, though. If my death could potentially pave the way for my father's murderer to be brought to justice, then it would be worth it. I just wanted there to be peace for my family, even if it meant my death. At least they would finally have some answers.

Thank God I had come up with the plan to leave Alex that note. It would be my fail-safe. It would also be my way of saying sorry… and goodbye to the man I once thought would be with me for the rest of my life. I hoped that the note would bring him some sort of closure. If there was one thing that I learned over the past two years, it was how important finding peace was after the death of a loved one. I would want that for Alex more than anything. I wanted that for my mom, too. Tonight my mother would find out what has been going on, one way or another. I just hoped that it would be because I was telling her about it over dinner rather than her reading it on a piece of paper. I tried to clear my mind. I pulled myself together and started getting ready for work.

As badly as I wanted to sit and think, instead of spending an hour primping, I knew that people would notice if my appearance was disheveled. If someone approached me to ask what was wrong, I would probably not be able to hold my emotions in. I needed to try to fly under the radar. It was best to look as if it were just another day at the office. I brushed and straightened my hair. I pulled the top half of my hair back and pinned it in place. It would be less distracting that way. I sat at my vanity and applied my makeup. My regimen was fairly quick. I liked to keep it light at the office as to look more professional. Once I was finished, I ventured into my closet. I wanted to wear something simple. Minimal was definitely the way to go today. I pulled on a pair of black slacks and my favorite pink sweater. It had been a Christmas gift from my dad a few years ago. It was appropriate for work and it would be a comfort to have something from him with me today. I threw on my usual black pumps, took one last glimpse in the mirror, and rushed out of the house.

I made sure to leave the door unlocked when I left my house. Good thing I lived in a safe neighborhood. I had instructed my mom to come in and make herself at home when she got here. I told her that there might be a chance that she would beat me home from work. Hopefully, it would be safe there. I did not know what Xavier's men would be capable of. Would they go to my house and kill anyone who was close to me? Would my mom just be in the wrong place at the wrong time? I hoped that neither of those would become reality. I tried to push those thoughts out of my mind and calm my nerves on my way to work. I would have to try hard to not lose control with Xavier. If I was frantic, he could easily play on my emotions. I needed to be the one dominating the conversation for once. I had to make him see that I was serious and wouldn't back down until he gave in to my demands.

I marched into the office with my head held high. I said hello to Janelle and proceeded through the door that led to the offices. I usually stopped for a few moments to chat with her about how our weekends had been. Janelle always seemed to have a fun story to tell. She was tall, blonde, and beautiful, so it was no surprise to me that her stories were usually about lustfully crazy men and the lengths that they had gone to trying to get her attention. I couldn't always relate to her endeavors, but I was amused with her stories nonetheless. Something about them inspired the writer inside of me. Janelle's life experiences could easily fill a novel and she was only 25. I wasn't much younger than her, but I knew that I wouldn't have tales like hers when I reach that age. There was no time to stop and chat with her today, though, as I was on a mission.

I decided to stop by my office first. Once I closed the door behind me and dropped my things on the desk, I glanced at the oversized clock hanging on the wall. It was 7:45, which meant I had fifteen minutes to mentally prepare myself before the staff meeting started. All I had to do was keep my cool during the meeting. Perhaps if I made no real eye contact with Xavier and spoke only of the publicity news I had, I would be fine. I sat down in the office chair and tried to calm my nerves. I kept repeating motivational statements in my head. Maybe when I made it to the meeting I should try picturing everyone in their underwear. I always heard that helped when you were nervous. It was a silly thought, but I was willing to try anything as long as it kept me from freaking out. I closed my eyes and tried to imagine that I was in a calmer place, envisioning myself lounging in a chair on the coast of some foreign island. An ice-cold margarita in my hand and no other sound but the ocean waves crashing in front of me. I could almost taste the salt in the air. Just as I was drifting away into my imaginary paradise, Martin was knocking on my door.

"Everyone is on their way to the conference room, Amy. I thought that perhaps I could escort you there."

"Of course you can, Martin." I tried to smile without showing the intense apprehension I was feeling. I stood up, pushed in my chair, and made my way to the conference room. I took one last deep breath and entered the room, keeping my head down. I strode quickly to my usual spot beside Xavier and immediately opened my notes. I pretended to be reading what I had written down. Hopefully, it would just appear as if I were preparing myself rather than avoiding eye contact with anyone.

The meeting was off to its usual start. Xavier thanked everyone for being prompt and briefly spoke of any weekend news that was worth mentioning.

The business was the same as always… profits still slowly climbing and more progress was being made in the drug trials. The head of the pharmaceutical research branch went over the newest drug that was being tested. It was supposed to be a breakthrough for the treatment of cystic fibrosis. So far, the results from the double-blind study were showing to be a raving success. The patients showed improvement in their symptoms. This research went hand in hand with what the stem cell research team was doing. The head of that department spoke of their developments as well. This would all be fantastic for the company's image down the road. That, of course, brought them to my news.

"I am in the progress of getting a major television news station to air a piece on Nectar Corp. It is too early to mention which company it is, but I am hoping that we would be able to get a primetime placement. If it works out, it is possible that it could be broadcast worldwide." I said as I tried to sound enthusiastic.

"That is fantastic, my dear! I knew you would be able to work wonders here. You show so much of the drive and initiative your father had." Xavier announced.

Everything about that statement made me want to come out of my skin! Just who did he think he was? Calling me pet names and referencing my father? My father would still be here today if it weren't for him! My life would be fine, and my family would be happy like we should be if he hadn't wrecked our dreams. I had to calm myself down. The last thing I wanted to do was cause a scene in front of all of my colleagues. There would be too many witnesses and they would call security on me for sure! I took a deep breath and mentally counted to three before I allowed myself to respond. I plastered a fake smile on my face and continued with my part of the meeting.

"Thank you, Xavier. I am happy that you are pleased with the progress."

The meeting continued for just a few more minutes. Xavier instructed all department heads to have their weekly reports to him by noon today and then wished everyone success with their projects for the week. After that, he dismissed everyone. I was so nervous that I was almost ready to back out of my plan, but I knew I had already come too far just to forget it.

"Xavier? If you have a spare moment, could we speak in your office?"

"Of course, Amy. I was just going there now. Why don't you follow me?"

I took a big gulp and followed him down the hall. I made a mental note of everyone who was in the general area. I wanted to know who would be in earshot of what I was going to say. There didn't need to be too many spectators. I knew that Xavier would use anything he could as leverage and I did not want any of these innocent people getting caught up in this mess. Luckily though, we were almost completely alone. The only people who remained in the wing were Martin Gilchrist and a woman from accounting, who was speaking in Martin's office. Just as Xavier and I walked by, Martin shut his office door. This was a good thing, I thought to myself. It meant that they would be less likely to hear anything that was going on in Xavier's office. Just a few more paces and we would be in his office. This was it, the moment that I had been waiting almost two years for. I followed Xavier inside of his office and closed the door behind me. We each took a seat.

"So to what do I own this pleasure, Amy?"

"Well, to be perfectly honest Xavier, I wouldn't call any of it a pleasure. It is about my father."

"Your father? Please, do go on." The look on his face seemed a bit perplexed.

"For the past two years, I have been struggling with the mystery surrounding my father's death. It has torn my family apart. Not to mention the toll that it has taken on my personal life."

"I am deeply sorry to hear that. Thomas's death was a serious blow to the scientific community. We were all saddened when we heard of the news."

"Yes, I'm sure many people were saddened. Anyway, after the authorities found his body, I went to my mother's house to clear out his things. That was the last thing that she needed to be dealing with. I boxed up his clothes and emptied his home office. I threw almost everything I found away. Most of it was of no real value anyhow. Just papers, copies, and old magazines. I did keep one thing, though. It was a little notebook I found that seemed to be hidden amongst the mess. I took it home and read it when I was alone. Do you have any idea what he wrote about in it?"

"I haven't the slightest. Something about a research idea or something, I presume. I think that is about all we scientists ever write about." he said with a disgusting chuckle.

"I guess that is one way of looking at it. Most of it didn't make much sense to me, but two things were mentioned consistently. Your name and immortality. This piqued my interest quite a bit. So, I got this job here and waited until the time was right. That time was last Friday at about 12:30. That is the precise moment that I found something rather interesting in your office. So, my question to you, Mr. Holland, is what role did you play in my father's death?"

Silence and anger filled the room. Normally I

would be scared, but I was filled with far too much rage for fear to be a factor now. My voice had been steady and my cheeks were flushed with anger. Tears were burning at the back of my eyes. I had been waiting for this moment for two long years. I decided that no matter what the outcome would be today, this very moment was worth it. The look on Xavier's face said it all. It was a mix between anger and shock. I was relishing the moment. I was salivating in suspense at what he was about to say to me.

"I assume this means you found *my* notebook also. It is nothing like you think it is and I don't feel that I owe you an explanation. You were the one that was snooping in my office, after all. I will explain it to you, though. It seems that otherwise, we will be at some sort of impasse. That is something that I do not have any interest in.

When I first started toying around with the idea of immortality, I went to your father for help. He was the smartest man I knew. You can imagine my frustration when he gave me no response at all. No look, no comment, nothing. I gave him a few days and finally paid him a visit when I still had not heard from him. I explained to him what my motives were. I assumed he must have thought that I was power hunger or something like that. They were not for power or fame at all. I described it to him exactly the way I did to you. What if his wife, your mother, had cancer and this could give her a second chance at life? Both of my parents died of cancer before they were able to see any of their accomplishments be recognized by anyone. I couldn't do anything but sit there and watch them die! So, he began to see where I was coming from and agreed to help me in any way he could, as long as I kept his name out of it. He didn't want to be associated with the stigma this would bring.

We made plans to meet three days later for a brainstorming session, but the next day he was reported missing. I swear to you Amy, I had nothing to do with it. Your father was one of my closest friends. I cried for days when I learned of his death. He was like a mentor to me, especially once my parents were gone."

"I don't buy it, Xavier. What if he had said no, what then? According to your notebook, his family was his soft spot. It seems to me that you had something sinister planned. Especially if he had told you that he wanted nothing to do with your immortality research. So why should I believe you? How do I know that he didn't tell you to screw off and you killed him because of it?"

"I don't know what to tell you, Amy. I am not an evil man. What you read was just my desperation and fear. How many times have you said something that you didn't mean? Have you ever made a threat that you knew you would never carry out? I *loved* your dad. I would never have hurt him. There were many times we disagreed on things, but I still respected him and his opinion. He was a brilliant man, and I would do anything to have him back."

I sat in silence for a moment. Xavier was slumped in his chair with tears in his eyes. I never expected that. At no time when I was playing through scenarios in my head did I think of him as a kind-hearted man who *loved* my father. He seemed genuinely pained that he was being accused of having any ill will toward him. I didn't know what to think. This was not the reaction I was expecting him to have.

"Then who would do such a thing, Xavier? For the past two years, you are the only person that I have considered as a suspect. If it wasn't you, who else is there?" I pleaded, so desperately, on the verge of tears. I was still accusing him, but I think I was also asking for help. This was closure that I needed so badly.

"I don't know. The timing was so precise that it made me think that it was related to the immortality research. In the beginning, I suspected that old boyfriend of yours. No one else had been as vocal about what we were doing as Alex was."

I was shocked. He just referred to Alex as my

boyfriend. How did Xavier know that Alex and I had been together? We had always kept our relationship so private.

"Don't look so surprised Amy. I did my research on you, too. I figured the fact that you two were no longer an item might fuel the fire for you to undo what he had done to our image. That is one of the reasons that I was so willing to hire you. Besides, having you here has been like getting a small piece of your father back in my life. You don't know how wonderful you have made me feel."

"I don't know what to say here, Xavier. I am sorry I never mentioned my connection with Alex. I thought it would complicate things, not to mention how it could possibly make me look. I am sure you can understand why I didn't. Do you still suspect him?"

"Of course I understand and no, I don't think he killed Thomas. He hates us for what we are doing, but I don't think he would ever harm someone because of it. I think he is all talk. Just virtue signaling, but no willingness to back anything up. To be honest, I don't know who it could be. I don't know who else could know about our research enough to be angry about it. Have you mentioned any of this to your family?"

"No, I haven't. Our relationships have become

pretty distant. I see my mother occasionally, but I never see my brother James. I don't think that they would even understand any of this if I told them. My mother would just get upset and James never did seem to have much of an interest in what dad did. He never spoke much about dad after he died. Once the grief started to wear off a little, he just disappeared altogether."

"It is probably for the best, then. Amy, I can't tell you have relieved I am to be having this discussion with you. I have kept my feelings about everything inside of me for so long. I don't have anyone close enough to talk to about this. I sure wasn't going to go to therapy. Maybe if we work together, we can figure this thing out. The police clearly didn't have any good leads or there would have been at least an arrest, don't you think?"

"I agree. I spoke with them a lot about the investigation and they never had much information. There had been no prints, no blood other than my father's and there were no witnesses to be found. I think that they eventually just gave up."

"That is what I thought as well. I assume they questioned your family after the disappearance."

"Yes, they did. They questioned my mother and me once each and they spoke to James two or three times."

"Why did they speak to him so much?"

"I'm not that sure. He said that he thought it was because he was somewhat familiar with the area in which they found my father. James's ex-girlfriend lives in that area."

"I see. Well, my dear, I think we should try to get some actual work done today. Would you like to sit down after work tomorrow and discuss this? Maybe we can make some progress and come up with our own leads. It will probably be helpful to have two perspectives on this now."

"I would love that. I do have work I need to be doing if we want our piece aired anytime soon. I am so happy to know that you are on my side, Xavier. You don't know how relieved I am to know that I am not going to be in this alone anymore."

"As am I Amy."

Xavier and I both rose from our chairs and met each other with an embrace. Emotion surged through my body. I was relieved, excited, comforted, and bewildered all at the same time. I was so overwhelmed. I smiled up at Xavier and turned to walk out of his office. I made my way down the hallway and was still smiling when I sat down in my office chair. Our encounter had not gone at all as I had expected and *I* thanked God for that. Instead of being in danger with an enemy, I was now going to have help searching for answers from a new friend. It was such a great feeling to have someone in my corner once again. I hadn't had someone to be there for me like that since Alex left. And even he didn't seem like he was completely there for me many times.

Alex… I wanted to call him and tell him the amazing news. I wanted to tell him how relieved and fired up I was. He wouldn't care, though. He would probably just be disgusted that I had a positive reason to keep Xavier in my life. I imagined that Alex would just put a negative spin on things and I did not want any part of that right now. It would only bring me down. I wanted to enjoy my triumph. I would be happy to place calls to get good press for Nectar Corp today. I no longer had a reason to resent the work that I was doing. Now I wanted to do as much as I could for Xavier.

I buried myself in work for the rest of the afternoon. I wrote several versions of what I wanted to be covered on Nectar Corp's primetime special. I placed dozens of phone calls to members of the media. By the time my workday was coming to an end, I was exhausted. I had just gathered my things when Xavier appeared at my door.

"You look like you're ready to go. May I walk you to your car?"

"Sure Xavier, that would be great." I said with a

smile. I was so giddy about having a new friend. I grabbed my sweater and joined him in the hallway.

The walk to the parking lot was quiet, yet comfortable in a strange way. I opened the door to my car and hopped in. Xavier stopped me before I had a chance to shut my door.

"Look, I know this may sound a bit strange, but it needs to be said. I feel very protective of you. I have grown quite fond of you over these past few weeks. Your father was killed over this business, and I don't want the same fate for you. Please take extra precautions to take care of yourself and call my cell phone if you *ever* feel you are in danger."

I was a bit taken aback by his announcement, but it pleased me to know that someone was willing to look out for me. On the other hand, this could all be misdirection. I had to keep in mind that he could still be the one responsible. My enemy. I needed to be smart about the way I handled this evolving situation.

"Absolutely. I really appreciate that, Xavier."

"Ok then. Have a safe night and I will see you tomorrow."

"Same to you."

I pulled out of my parking spot and merged into traffic. The drive home was a bit nerve-racking. The thought of my dad being killed over things that I had seen firsthand made me uneasy. I kept looking over my shoulder the entire drive home. Relief surged through me when I pulled onto my street and saw my mom's car parked in front of my house. I had almost forgotten that I had invited her over for dinner. What was I going to say to her? There was no way that I could keep this information to myself. I was busting at the seams as it was. It was too late to debate this now I thought to myself as I parked my car. I would just have to see what happens.

"Hi, mom!" I shouted as I walked through the front door.

"Hi, my baby girl! I've missed you so much. How are you?" she met me with what felt like the tightest hug I have ever had.

"I'm doing really well. I've been working with a new company for the past few weeks and I like it a lot. I will tell you more about it after dinner. You look, great mom. How have you been?"

"Oh, you know how it is. I still have my bad days, but overall there have been more good days than anything else."

"That's good to hear. How is James? I haven't spoken with him in such a long time."

"That makes two of us. No matter how hard I try to get in touch with him, it seems like I never can, He doesn't even return my calls these days. I don't know what is going on with him. I just keep telling myself, Joan, you have to let him grieve in his own way."

"I don't know. I wish he wouldn't neglect you like that, though. He could at least call."

"I'm sure it is still hard for him, dear. He always thought he would have a chance to be closer with your father down the road and that chance was taken away. I imagine he is filled with much regret."

"I see what you mean. Well, have a seat at the dinner table. I popped a roast in the crock-pot before I left for work this morning. It should be ready to serve. I'll go get it dished up for us."

I trotted into the kitchen to get dinner plated. I felt so at ease at the moment, especially since my mom was here now. I filled each plate with slices of roast and vegetables and entered the dining room.

"Dinner is served!" I said cheerfully.

We sat together at the table and enjoyed eating our meal together in silence. I waited until we had both cleared our plates before I spoke up.

"Let's go have a seat in the living room. I will clean this mess up later. We have a lot to talk about. Plus, I ate way too much and I need to stretch out." I stood up with a laugh and led my mother into the living room. We each took a seat on opposite ends of the couch.

"Mom, I need to tell you about the company I have been working for the past few weeks."

"Ok. I hope this isn't going to end badly, Amy. I don't know if I can take much bad news right now. Considering this is the first I'm hearing about this job, I can't help but assume you aren't about to tell me that you won employee of the month. When did you leave the newspaper?"

"It's not bad news mom, don't worry. I requested a leave of absence at the newspaper a few weeks ago. Right before I started my new job. The place I have been working is called Nectar Corp. Have you ever heard of it?"

"Yes, I have. That is the company your father's friend Xavier works for."

"You know Xavier Holland? I never heard either of you mention him before."

"He and your father were very close, but your father liked to keep his professional life separate from his personal life. He never wanted you kids mixed up in his world of playing mad scientist. I made it a point to never bring any of it up."

"Did you ever suspect that Xavier might have played a role in dad's death?"

"Oh my God. No, never. Why?"

"Well, when I was clearing dad's things out of the house, I found one of his notebooks. I kept it and read it once I was at home. There were so many things written about Xavier. Most of them were also about immortality. The things were written in such a way that it seemed like dad was frightened when he wrote them. Most of it was not even legible. It made me feel as if it were Xavier that had frightened him."

"Wait, did you say immortality?"

"Yes. I didn't understand either, mom. That's why I got the job at Nectar Corp. I had convinced myself that Xavier was the person behind dad's death. I took a hiatus from the newspaper and got myself a job as a PR representative for his company. My goal was to find evidence of my theory once I was on the inside."

"Did… did you find anything?"

"Yes, I did. I found a notebook hidden in Xavier's office. It spoke of immortality and dad. He asked dad for his help with research and seemed to be going mad when dad wouldn't give him an answer."

"I just don't know what to say… they always seemed to have so much love for each other. Did you find anything else?"

"No, but I confronted Xavier about it today."

"What? Amy, you could have gotten yourself killed! What did he say? What happened?"

"He explained to me that he went to see dad a few days after he asked for his help. He explained to dad why he wanted to find a way to create immortality and that dad finally agreed to help him. They made plans to meet a few days later to brainstorm. The next day is when you reported him missing."

"Oh my God. I can't believe that your father would agree to such a crazy thing! Do you still believe he is behind it?"

"No, not anymore. He cried when he spoke of how much he loved dad. I don't think there is any way he could have killed him. He agreed to try to help me find out who did, though. I know you won't want me to do any of this mom, but I have to. I have to solve this once and for all. It is the only way I can ever find any peace. Xavier wants to do the same. He seems so genuinely saddened by dad's death also. We want to help each other."

"Amy, I love you. I am not going to tell you not to do this. I know it is something that you have to do. Honestly, it will help me too if we can figure this whole thing out. I think you are in good hands with Xavier. He was always kind to me, and I know how much your dad valued his friendship. Just please be careful.”

"I will mom. If you speak to James, please don't tell him about any of this. I don't think he would understand. Xavier probably wouldn't even want me telling you. He doesn't want anyone to know about the research going on with immortality. I'm sure you can understand why.”

"Of course. How does Alex feel about all of this? I'm sure he can't be happy about it. Does he understand?”

"Oh, that's right.” I started blinking back tears. "Actually, he broke up with me. He said that he couldn't stand by and watch while I negated all of the bad things he had published about Xavier. I told him I had no choice but to do what I was doing, so we went our separate ways.” I couldn't blink the tears back anymore. My heart hurt too bad and there was something so comforting about my mom's presence.

"Oh my baby girl, I am so sorry to hear that. I know how much he meant to you. You seemed so perfect for each other. I wish you would have told me. Breakups are hard and I should have been there for you.”

"It is ok, mom. The rewards I see in my future are worth the loss. It has torn me apart, though. I can't lie. It's gotta get easier, right?”

"Well, I am glad to see you have such a positive

outlook on the situation now. And yes, of course, it will get easier. These things just take time."

"Thanks. It's getting late; I know you need to get home mom. Let me walk you to your car. I need some fresh air anyway."

I got up and helped my mother gather her things. I opened the front door and walked mom to her car. Truthfully, I didn't want her to leave. She didn't need to sit and watch me cry all night, though. A pity party was not going to do either of us any good. She was still dealing with her own emotions. I knew how much she missed my dad. I still didn't know if she was in danger either. It would be safer for her if she wasn't around me.

"Thank you, for everything Amy. I appreciate how much you are doing to solve the mystery of your father's passing. You will never know how much it means to me. I really do need closure. It won't ever bring him back, but perhaps it will help. I love you, sweetheart."

"Of course, mom. I love you and I will see you soon. Have a safe drive home. Call or text me when you get there, or I will worry."

I kissed my mom on the forehead and stood on the front porch, watching while she drove away. When I could no longer see her taillights, I went back inside the house. I closed the door and locked it behind me. I closed the blinds and locked all of the windows. Xavier made me promise him that I would take extra precautions to safeguard myself and I wasn't about to slip up on that promise. I couldn't take any chances. Once everything was secure, I headed upstairs. I took a long hot shower and hopped into bed. Sleep always came so much easier after I showered. Something about the cleanliness made me feel at ease. I smiled as I thought about all of the peace that today had brought to me. Tonight would be the first night in a long time that I would be able to sleep soundly.

CHAPTER EIGHT

I was still smiling when I awoke the next morning. Last night my dreams were calm, even peaceful. When was the last time I was able to say that? Too long to remember. It has been so long. I lingered in bed as I replayed one of the dreams over in my mind. I concentrated hard to remember as many details as I could.

I was walking in the park with a man whose face I could not see. His presence felt warm... like a blanket fresh out of the dryer. I looked into the eyes of everyone I saw. There were mothers and fathers with their children and several couples walking hand in hand. There was a blissful smile on my face. I felt calm and sure of myself amidst all of the chaos around me. The unknown man and I strode side by side down the concrete path ahead of us. It was a uniquely beautiful day. The sun was shining and there was a cool breeze. I closed my eyes and listened to the birds chirping. It was a harmonious melody that brought an even bigger smile to my face. The grass was the most blazing shade of green that I had ever seen. It was brilliant. There were rows of blooming flowers separating the sidewalk from the grass. Today, the park looked like a scene from a calendar.

"How do you feel knowing you will be alive after all of these people have passed?" the still unknown man asked me with a slight chuckle.

"Surprisingly fine. It's as if I have a new lease on life… a very long life. It is strange to think about, though. I suppose that only time will tell whether or not I will be able to mentally handle it. It could go either way." I replied.

I was beautiful in my dream. It felt as if it was far in the future, yet my appearance remained unchanged. I looked like an ageless version of myself. There were no blemishes or laugh lines. I was flawless. We reached the end of the path and turned to look at each other. I could finally see his face. It was Xavier. He smiled down at me and brushed a piece of hair out of my face.

"Saving you was the best decision I have ever made. May you enjoy eternal life, my dear." He smiled a smile I had never

seen before. I could feel the sincerity in my heart.

And the dream was over.

What did that mean? I always hate this moment when I first wake up. I go over the dreams I have had and try to decide if any of them are a foretelling of my future. I hope this dream was not a glimpse into my future. I rationalized that it was just my subconscious weaving through all of my thoughts and experiences from the past few weeks. It was just a culmination of the information overload happening in my brain.

I got out of bed and started getting ready for work. I straightened my hair and put on makeup. It was nice to make an effort on myself again. I glanced up at the clock and realized that I had lost track of time. How did that happen? I raced to my room and threw on some work clothes. I grabbed a bottle of water out of the refrigerator and practically ran out of the house.

I was secretly giddy when I got to work and found Xavier waiting in my office with a cup of coffee. I think I was still feeling the mood of the dream I had. Granted, I did feel pretty awkward as well. I smiled and took the cup of coffee out of his hand. It was certainly needed.

"Thank you so much! This is exactly what I need this morning. I can't believe I managed to make it here on time."

"No problem at all. Did you oversleep?"

"Kind of. Have you ever had a dream that was just so vivid that you laid in bed and thought about it?"

"Yes, I believe I have. It must have been quite the dream."

"It was. Anyway, before I knew it, it was time to leave. Thankfully, there wasn't much traffic. It must be a holiday; there weren't any school busses or minivans in the carpool lanes."

"It is a teacher planning day, I believe. Martin took the day off because his little ones are at home. That's what happens when you don't read your kid's calendar… you don't know when you need a sitter." He chuckled, so I didn't think he was actually annoyed about the situation.

"That was nice of you to give him the day off. You must be anticipating a light workload."

"Somewhat. I'm sure you have a lot on your plate, though. Are you still interested in discussing your father after work this evening?" His eyes darted away from mine when he asked. Was he nervous?

"Absolutely. I do have a lot to do around here today. It will be nice to get out afterward."

"Ok. I guess I'll leave you to it, then. I will check

on you later this afternoon to discuss dinner arrangements."

"Sounds good to me. See you later then."

I couldn't wipe the ridiculous smile off of my face. What was wrong with me? I guess that it was just nice to not have the idea of Xavier murdering my father hanging over my head all day. It would be a nice change of pace to genuinely want to get this place some good press. Now that I had good motivation, who knows how much I could accomplish.

Motivation is what I was going to need to get me through this day. I had so much to do. First, I decided to make a list of everyone I needed to call. I should also sit and write exactly what I want to be covered in our prime time special. Who should I pick for the spokesperson? My gut was telling me to go with Martin. I initially considered asking Xavier to do it, but I thought too many people associate him with a negative image right now. Plus, it would be impossible not to like Martin Gilchrist. He had been one of the most caring individuals that I have come across recently. I think that America would love him just as much as I did.

By the time I finished placing my calls and writing out my prime time thoughts, it was nearly three o'clock. I could probably find enough work to take up my last hour, but I decided instead to reward myself with an hour of relaxation. So, I took a walk out front and chatted with Janelle for a while. I stretched out the walk back to my office and managed to only have 30 minutes of workday left by the time I got there. Changing the background on my laptop and playing around with the color scheme ought to take up the rest of the time.

It was almost four o'clock when Xavier showed up at my door. I was surprised at the butterflies in my stomach, but it should've been expected. After all, I was about to make some progress in figuring out the big unsolved mystery of my life. If I wasn't nervous, it would be alarming.

"You're still up for going out, right?" Xavier asked with a smile that I could get used to seeing around here.

"Of course I am. What did you have in mind?"

"There's a quiet restaurant called Stuffed about 20 minutes from here. The prices are pretty cheap, but the food is amazing. I promise you will love it."

"That's fine with me. I've heard of that place before, but never stopped to check it out. We will see if it lives up to its name. I am super hungry. Can I just follow you there?"

"No problem."

Xavier walked with me to the parking lot and said a quick "I'll see you there" before we pulled away. I was happy to find that the 20-minute drive was in the direction of my house. It would be a quick trip home tonight.

We pulled into the parking lot Stuffed and I realized why I had never stopped before. It was a shock that there was even a restaurant in this strip. For starters, almost every building appeared to be very run down. The location was shady, but if Xavier said it was good, I had no choice but to believe him. Plus, I really was starving.

"I was starting to wonder just where you were leading me. I would never have guessed that there would be a restaurant here." I said with a chuckle.

"The neighborhood used to be better. I am surprised that this place still manages to stay open. I guess that the people who know about it like it so much that they keep coming back no matter what."

"Yeah, that makes sense. After you." I motioned for the door and followed him in. The place was beautiful on the inside. Dark cherry wood tables between what looked to be very comfortable booth seats. The lighting was just dim enough to be comfortable but not romantic. Based on the outside, the interior was a welcomed surprise.

Xavier and I got seated and I ordered right away.

I couldn't believe how hungry I was. I figured I wouldn't have much of an appetite considering how nervous I had become. If you would have told me a week ago that I would be having dinner with Xavier Holland today I would have laughed. Like, a hearty belly laugh. Now that it was happening, I had so many thoughts filling my head it was hard not to blurt them out. The good thing about that was at least I would make a good conversationalist.

"I am really excited that we are doing this. It would help me so much to be able to put some of the pieces of this puzzle together." And it truly was helpful. I was so happy at the thought of figuring out my father's last moments on this earth. Hopefully, this wouldn't go south.

"I feel the same. In a way, these past few weeks I have felt as if I had a bit of Thomas back. You are like your father in many ways. Just your presence has the same energy as his. He was such an important part of my life."

"That means a lot to me. Thank you."

"It's my pleasure. Let me ask you... if your father hadn't passed away, would you have tried to find a place in this business? Probably not, I'm guessing."

"Honestly, I don't think so. I have always been fascinated with science and the discoveries that have been and can be made, but I also wanted to do something of my own. I always had a fear that if I tried to be part of this, people would assume that I got where I was because of who my father was. I didn't want that for myself. Not that I am somewhat involved, though, I do enjoy being a part of it."

"I certainly understand where you are coming from. My father was also a scientist and I had to deal with that type of opposition a lot when I first got into the business. I still do. I will admit, part of where I am at is because of who my father was. That doesn't mean I'm not worthy of it, though. I worked my ass off to prove to everyone that I *did* deserve to be where I was."

"What kind of scarifies did you have to make?" As soon as I asked the question, I realized how snarky it came out. Almost like I didn't think he would have had to make any sacrifices. That's not the way I meant it, though.

"A lot that I didn't want to. I mean, look at me. I am 27 years old, I have no girlfriend, no children… hell, I have never even had a very serious relationship. Sometimes I envy the hell out of some of the people I used to be friends with. They are in relationships, they do things on Friday nights, and they have lives. I have given all of that up to get where I am now."

"Wow. I am sorry to hear that, Xavier. It is hard to make those kinds of sacrifices. Those who don't have to will never understand. I guess we just have to hope in the end that it is worth it." I honestly didn't know what to say to that. I wasn't surprised at the things he's had to give up. I could always see the loneliness in his eyes. It was something I could relate to these days. Nothing like spending a Friday night on your couch, alone, with a carton of ice cream and a spoon. I didn't tell him any of that, though. The last thing a lonely person wants is someone to point out is that people can tell that they *are* that lonely.

Our food arrived after a few moments of awkward silence. Thankful that there was now a reason to be silent, I dug in. I was immediately happy with my choice. It was easily the best chicken and dumplings that I ever had. It even had my favorite kind of dumplings. The biscuit kind, not the big noodles. But after about ten minutes of silently eating, I decided to speak up.

"So, what are your last memories with my father?" I decided to be assertive and start the discussion that we were here to have. This needed to start moving in the right direction. This wasn't a date. I was there for answers.

"Well, you obviously know about my proposition and that I finally went to see him. The night of the visit was such a high point in my life. I mean, the scientist I have tried to model myself after for most of my career had just agreed to work with me on something big. Bigger than any other project I had ever worked on. I was on cloud nine. Your father and I spent that evening talking about different plans while we had a couple of drinks. It felt like a dream. After we came up with a few of what we thought were really strong ideas, we called it a night. We didn't have a plan yet, but things were headed in a good direction. He said that he was going to swing by your brother's house and then head home. That was the last time I ever saw him."

"Why was he going to see James?" I was confused.

Dad and James hadn't gotten along very well in a long time. They disagreed on so many things… especially science. I was honestly surprised to hear that he even knew where James lived. James never mentioned any of this. Something must have happened on his way there. I wonder if he even knew dad was coming over. At least I was establishing a timeline.

"I don't know, I didn't ask. He didn't talk about you guys very much. Why? Is that out of the ordinary?"

"Well, yes. You see, my dad and James never saw eye to eye. James thought that much of what dad did for a living was wrong. Several years ago when he had an opportunity to be part of a genetic mutation study, James was furious. He was convinced that the experiments that they were going to conduct 'went against nature.' Their relationship became very distant after that. Dad ended up taking on another project instead, but James didn't care. The damage was already done in his eyes. That was the pinnacle I guess."

"I had no idea. I bet he would have hit the roof if he had known about the newest endeavor."

"I'm sure he would have. I didn't talk to James about dad after that. He would get mad and say that I always took dad's side."

We both sat in uncomfortable silence for several minutes. I feared that we were thinking the same thing. Xavier was the first to break the silence.

"Did James ever mention their meeting to you?"

"No, he didn't. He told my mother and me that he hadn't spoken to dad in months. He had very little to say. We figured that he was feeling guilty because of that. Death brings out so many feelings of guilt and remorse. Is it possible that he didn't know dad was coming to see him?"

"I honestly can't say. Thomas never mentioned it being a surprise visit, but he didn't say that it was planned either. Your guess is as good as mine. As I said, he typically left family out of our conversations."

My head felt cluttered with thoughts and my heart began to race. It was getting hot. Did James have something to do with this? How could he have? Dad would have never told him about this. He didn't have time to anyway. James would never ask either. It must just be a fluke. Xavier could be trying to throw me off.

"I really don't think there is anything to be found with my brother. Is there anyone else who knew about what the two of you were planning? A partner or enemy?"

"Not really. This may be a tough subject to breach... but what do you think about Alex Cardwell? I know we have talked about hm before, but maybe it is worth taking another look at."

My heart had officially dropped into my stomach. Alex. Could he? Was I that stupid? I let out a long sigh.

"Definitely a tough one, but maybe necessary. I can say without a doubt that he hates you and almost everything he thinks you stand for. I never heard him say anything about my father unless I asked. Even then, it wasn't much. He knew I was sensitive. I must admit that I told him my theory about you..."

"Did you now? What were his remarks?" Xavier asked with one eyebrow raised.

"He told me that you were evil and things like that. He also told me that you would sacrifice someone's life in the name of science without a second thought. When I asked if he had ever heard of my dad being involved in any of it, he said no."

"Well, I can say that if he didn't know that your father was part of it, he is probably not guilty. If he did know, however, 'm not so sure. I know I have said that he seemed to be all talk, but maybe I was wrong. Everyone has a breaking point I suppose. For someone who claims to have such a strong moral compass, he can stoop pretty low."

"You know, it's strange to think about him like that. He helped me through such a terrible time in my life and now to think that he has cast me away *and* we are considering the thought that he might be behind my father's death. I just feel so hurt... and stupid. Honestly, I am starting to feel like one of those stupid girls on a Lifetime movie. You know, the kind that everyone get frustrated with because she is so oblivious?"

I couldn't believe that I was telling Xavier any of this. Sure, I didn't think that he was my enemy anymore, but why was I confiding in him? What a weird day this had been. I was ready for it to be over. My brain hurt.

"Is there anyone else who knew about your

research?" Truth be told, I was feeling a bit desperate to find another suspect that didn't include someone I loved. "Is there an old girlfriend or something?"

"No, unfortunately there is no girlfriend, past or present to speak of. There is no one else that I can think of at the moment."

I don't know why, but that statement made me feel so sorry for Xavier. He had to give up so much for his work that it seemed he had completely sacrificed his happiness. Not to mention, he was such a good looking man. It was hard to believe he was on the 40 year old virgin course.

"Well, I think we have made good progress, don't you Amy?" He seemed ready to escape after the mention of never having a girlfriend. I didn't blame him. I was feeling awkward after my confessions as well.

"I do. Wanna get out of here? I am ready for a shower and some sleep." I just needed some time to myself. I had a lot to think about.

We walked to the parking lot and Xavier made sure I got in my car and buckled up.

"Amy, I really enjoyed this tonight. Even though we were discussing some unhappy subject matter. It's just nice to spend time with someone that isn't within the walls of Nectar."

"I had a good time too. I will see you in the morning, Xavier." I started my car and pulled away from the restaurant. I saw him do the same and go in the direction of what I assumed was his house. Either way, it was the opposite direction.

And at that moment, my heart knew exactly how he felt... empty. I guess misery really did love company. Boy did I need to get home and clear my head. This was all just too much. Tears were starting to well up in my eyes. I cried way too much these days.

CHAPTER NINE

I decided that I needed to confront James before I had even gone to sleep last night. I needed to know if he had an alibi for that night. Did he know that dad was coming to visit him? The more I sat and thought about things, the sicker my stomach began to feel. So many things just fell into place when I imagined him as the murderer. Just the thought of it made me want to cry. But what did he have to gain?

What I wanted to do was call in sick, but I couldn't do that. Xavier would know that something was wrong, and I wasn't ready to talk about my brother being a cold-blooded murderer just yet. I needed to remember that Xavier could still be the murderer too. I was afraid that if I told Xavier about my suspicions, he would take it farther than I was ready to. This had to be done in my own time and way. So I forced myself to get ready for work and practiced painting on my smile.

I was so deep in thought that I was surprised when I found myself pulling into Nectar Corp's parking lot. I must have been so consumed... I didn't even remember leaving my house, let alone driving through morning traffic. Hopefully, I didn't run any red lights. I turned my cd player to a song that would pump me up and put me in the right mood to get me through the day. I stopped when I found a suitable song and mentally went over my to-do list. I tried to pack it full of things that would occupy my time. As the song was ending I grabbed my things and turned off the car.

Just as I would any other day, I made a pit stop at Janelle's desk. As usual, she had fun-filled stories of her drunken escapades. It was kind of nice to be able to vicariously live through her. I would never be brazened enough to live the way she did, but she made it fun to dream.

I eventually made my way to my office and wasn't entirely surprised to find Xavier waiting for me there.

"Isn't it illegal to break into someone else's office?" I tried to say with a chuckle. Ok, maybe it came out with a flirty tone. What was wrong with me?

"I suppose… but when you own the company you tend to get away with things."

"One of the perks I imagine." I couldn't help but go along with him. It was easy being bitchy when I thought that Xavier was a bad person, but now that he had opened up to me, I couldn't be anything but nice to him. That's what was going to make today so difficult for me.

Before I made any rash decisions, maybe I should talk to someone neutral. In the old days, I would call Julie. She was my partner in crime. Birthdays, holidays, weekends… we were always together.

It was so hard after dad died. I shut everyone out, even Julie. After I started to cope, I met Alex and was completely immersed in our relationship. The more time passed, the more awkward and crappy I felt for essentially abandoning our friendship. She probably would have understood, but I don't know.

There was no one else I could turn to about it. Mom was too close to the situation. James was a suspect. No one at Nectar Corp could be trusted. She was the only one.

I decided to face the situation and call her. The

worst that could happen was her hanging up on me. So, I pulled out my cell phone and dialed her number. Even if I didn't have her info saved on my phone anymore, I could never forget her number. 221-2212. I was always jealous that it was so easy.

To my surprise and delight, she answered *and* sounded genuinely happy to be hearing from me. I felt relieved when she didn't ask for an explanation either.

"Amy! Oh my gosh, it is so good to hear your voice. It's like Christmas!" I forgot just how much I loved her peppy spirit. It was refreshing.

After a quick but not rushed exchange of pleasantries, I knew I needed to get down to business, I gave her a brief as possible run down of dad's death, my suspicion and subsequent change of heart about Xavier, and my current dilemma with James.

"Shit Amy. This is a mess. I mean, how are you even coping? And do you think Alex Cardwell plays into any of this?"

"Alex?" I heard a nervous laugh slip out when I said his name. How did she know about Alex? I had purposely left him out of my recap.

"Oh please girl. Do you really think I was gonna let you fade away completely? No way. I kept my eyes open. How else was I gonna know if my bestie was ok?"

"I should have known… and I don't know about Alex. I don't think he is part of anything, I guess."

"Yes, you should have. If you want my honest opinion, I think you should keep a close eye on this Xavier guy. He could be playing you. And call your brother before this grows into something ugly. I know you won't be able to let it go otherwise."

"You're right. I won't. I started to feel like I was going crazy… paranoid about everything. Thank you for talking me through it, Julie. I've really missed your insight."

"You are always so welcome. BUT, don't let this be our only call for a year. I worry about you. Plus, I am super curious about all of this now. Let me know what you find out and if I can help."

As we hung up, I felt relieved. Just hearing Julie's voice made me feel better. Not to mention getting some unbiased advice. Now I knew what I needed to do. I shouldn't have let so much time pass before calling her.

I couldn't wait any longer, I needed to call James. I hadn't spoken to him in -months, so I hoped it would just seem like his little sister checking in. As I dialed his number my stomach fluttered with nerves.

"Hey, Amy. What's up?"

"Hey, big brother. How are you?"

"I can't complain too much. It is good to hear your voice."

"Same here. Look, I was hoping you had some free time this week to meet me for lunch or something."

"Sure, I can make time for that. Is something wrong?"

"No, I just miss my brother." I hoped that he believed me. Did my tone of voice give something away?

"Ok, are you free for dinner tomorrow night?"

"I am. Can we make it someplace close to my house?"

"Sure. How about that restaurant on the corner of 5th St and Michigan Ave? You know, the shitty looking one."

That was the restaurant Xavier and I went to last night. I hate coincidences.

"That is perfect. See you at 7?"

"Sounds good, sis. See you tomorrow."

I hung up the phone and almost started to cry. I wished that this could just be a happy meeting to reconnect with each other. It was the truth when I said that I missed my brother. I loved my brother, and I didn't want to accuse him of anything… especially killing our father. I was stuck in a mental (not to mention emotional) battle over the matter when Xavier walked into my office.

"Hey. I don't want to make things weird, but I have really enjoyed spending time with you. I have been alone for so long. It is nice to have someone to talk to again."

I couldn't hold it in anymore and I began to sob. Xavier looked shocked and slightly horrified as he shut my door to give us privacy. That poor man didn't even know what he was walking into.

"I'm sorry, Amy. I should have kept my mouth shut. Just forget I said anything about it. It is inappropriate of me."

"No, it's not you Xavier. I did a lot of thinking when I got home last night. So many signs point to James and the thought kills me. I was on the phone with him right before you came in. I'm meeting him tomorrow night to 'catch up'. I need to try to feel him out or something. I don't mean to cry… it's just that I don't know what is going on in my life. One moment I think you are a killer and the next you are my friend. Now I suspect my brother of murdering my father. I feel like I am losing my mind."

Tears continued to stream down my face and Xavier came around my desk to hug me. I felt so calm, so safe in his arms. I almost didn't want him to let go. It had been so long since I had someone to hold me and try to comfort me. I didn't realize how much I missed that until now. Julie's reminder not to trust him flashed in my mind. I hated feeling this vulnerable.

"You don't have to apologize to me. To be perfectly honest, the possibility of your brother being a part of things was always in the back of my mind. I didn't think it was proper to say anything to you about it. Not yet anyway. Why didn't you say anything before now?"

I had already said way more than I wanted to about the situation, so I may as well not hold back now. What did I have to lose?

"I was afraid you may want to take things too far too quickly. I don't know what to feel about the situation. I just want to be able to take whatever action is needed, if any, at my own pace."

"I understand why you would think that. This is your brother, though. I will help however you need or want me to. Other than that, though, I will stay out of the way. I don't want to make this any harder on you than it must already be. I am always here to lean on though Amy." He kissed the top of my head.

I didn't know what else to say, so I just smiled and gave him another hug before he left my office. I was happy that he was ready to let me do this on my own, but also glad to know he was just a phone call away if I needed him.

If I needed him… that was a thought that scared me. For so long I had hated this man. Now I was afraid that I would start to need him. I wanted our relationship to be nothing but professional, but I was beginning to see Xavier in an entirely different light. I now saw the vulnerable and caring side of him. It was the side that showed me just how human he was. That was nothing like the man I once considered him to be.

I needed to try to push all of that to the side. All of my energy needed to be focused on James. I needed to ask the right questions without him thinking that I suspected him of anything. I knew James well enough to know that suspicion would send him running. It was time to throw myself into some paperwork and let the rest of my workday pass me by. It would be dinner time before I knew it.

So I worked vigorously for hours on press statements and publications on some of the positive things Nectar had accomplished within the last few weeks. Thankfully, there was a lot to cover because it kept me busy for the rest of the day. I had completely stopped looking at the clock when I started working on everything and I didn't look again until it was almost five. I was surprised because Xavier would normally have come by my office before it got this late. He was probably just giving me some space.

I packed all of my things into my briefcase and, in a complete role reversal, ventured out to find Xavier. I could have just left, but after saying goodbye to each other almost every day since I started working here it would feel weird to just slip out. Plus, I wanted him to keep tabs on me in case dinner with James this evening went awry. It is always a good idea to have a backup plan and Xavier was mine.

"Knock, knock." I stood in his doorway and waited for him to invite me in.

"Hey. It's not often that you make it down to this end of the offices. What time is it?" Xavier rubbed his eyes as he pushed his chair away from the desk.

"It's quitting time. I just wanted to say goodbye before I left for the day."

"If you can hang on for just a minute, I will walk out with you. I have done more than enough work today." He sounded tired.

I waited as he gathered his things and locked his office door. He put his hand on my back and began to lead me out of the building. I wished that I would feel this confident when I saw James.

CHAPTER TEN

Everything that happened from the time that I said goodbye to Xavier to the moment that I pulled up to the restaurant was a complete blur. I was shaking almost uncontrollably as I pulled my car into a parking spot. I turned the car off, took a few deep breaths, and went inside. The longer I sat there in the parking lot, the harder it would be to go inside. I didn't see James anywhere, so I asked for a table for two and waited to be seated. It was a short wait; only about ten minutes; and I shot James a text once I was in the booth letting him know that I got us a spot already. I picked up the menu and quickly scanned the dinner specials even though I knew I was too nervous to eat.

Should I order something? I would just be wasting money. My appetite was not going to miraculously return. Nothing on the menu looked good, but I didn't want to be rude. I never went to restaurants by myself. I always arrived with friends or a date. What was the proper etiquette?

My server was nice, but I could tell she was getting annoyed that after ten minutes I had yet to order any food. I barely even looked at the menu. It probably looked like I was loitering. So far, I had ordered a coke and gone through two refills. With nothing else to do with my nervous energy, I just kept drinking. I felt guilty, so I ordered a cobb salad with ranch dressing on the side that I had no intention of eating. What was taking James so long? I sent him another text and tried calling him. I didn't get a response to either attempt.

When James still hadn't shown up after nearly 45 minutes, I decided to leave. It was clear that I was being stood up by my own brother. Pathetic. The fact that he hadn't shown up was awfully telling. I paid for my soda and salad and was leaving a tip when my phone rang. Even though I had deleted the number out of my phone long ago, I recognized the caller. It was Alex. My heart instantly dropped to the bottom of my stomach. The urge to throw up and cry was immediate. Ugh, my heart.

"Hello?" I asked as I answered, trying to act as if I didn't already know who it was. I wanted him to think that I had completely forgotten about him after he dumped me when I needed him the most. It was what I should have done, after all. What could he want anyway? Did he see me here at the restaurant? I hoped not. I was sitting by myself looking woeful. I finished leaving my tip and tried to quickly make my way to the car.

"You aren't going to find the answers you are looking for, Amy." He said with an evil, sadistic tone that I had never heard him use before. His voice was different, but still Alex. Even through our breakup, he never sounded so mean… so cold. I could feel the hate radiating through the phone.

"Alex, what the hell are you talking about? Why are you even calling me? What answers? After all this time, are you seriously calling to harass me about what I am doing at Nectar Corp?" I was so nervous. My hands shook uncontrollably as I unlocked my car door, sat down, and struggled to shove the keys into the ignition.

"I know why you wanted to meet with James. He isn't coming, but I'm sure you figured that out by now. In fact, he is long gone at this point. He is far away from you and your new boyfriend. So, like I said, you aren't going to find the answer you are looking for. All you are going to find if you don't stop snooping around is more death. Watch your step, bitch." He made a kiss noise and that was it. He was gone.

Before I could even say another word, he had hung up. I instantly burst into tears. What was happening? This didn't even feel like real life anymore. It had to be some weird, realistic dream that I couldn't escape from. Was I really in a coma or something? I didn't feel safe sitting in my car alone. He knew I was at the restaurant waiting for James. Was he watching me right now? I wanted to drive away, but I couldn't.

My head was spinning with questions and confusion. Were he and James working together? Had he done something to James? This whole time, I never really imagined Alex being a part of things. Xavier and I had talked about it, but it my heat I didn't believe it would be him. He had been my boyfriend and the love of my life. Was he now going to be my enemy? Had he been this whole time ad I just didn't know it? I felt like I was going to hyperventilate.

It was official, nothing was as I thought it was. I didn't know what to think. My brain felt like spaghetti. If anyone knew exactly how I felt, they would probably have me committed. I knew someone who could help me sort it out, though. It was awfully late for an unexpected visit, but I had no other choice. I desperately needed someone to help me make sense of things. Not to mention the fact that I was now a bit too scared to go home.

Xavier looked disheveled and sleepy when he came to the door. He was wearing pajama pants and no shirt. He was in better shape than I would have expected a scientist to be. I certainly didn't expect to see defined abs.

"Are you ok, Amy? What's going on?" he asked while rubbing his eyes.

I started tearing up before I could even answer him. He just wrapped his arm around me and led me into the house. He locked the door behind us as I headed for the couch. I was so calm and collected on the drive over. Once I pulled myself together before leaving the restaurant at least. I was surprised that I fell apart at the first sight of him. That normally only happened with my mom. When he joined me on the couch, he had two glasses of water.

"Did your dinner not go well? Why didn't you call me?" he asked, handing me one of the glasses. I took a big gulp and tried to calm myself down. It helped.

"I don't know. I just felt like I needed to talk to

you in person. I am so sorry for showing up here unannounced. Now that I'm here, I feel a bit embarrassed. I just didn't know where else to go."

"No apologies needed. There is certainly no reason to be embarrassed. I want to help. I meant it when I said whatever you need. You are always welcome to come to me anytime you need something. Are you going to tell me what happened? Something clearly isn't okay."

"James never showed up tonight. That was humiliating enough, but it didn't stop there. As I was about to leave, Alex called me. He… he threatened me." It was hard to get the words out. Just to think about the love we shared in the past made this new reality hard to accept. I heard pure hatred in his voice. The only person that I had ever heard him use that tone about was Xavier. "He told me that I was not going find the answers I was looking for and I would only find more death if I didn't stop looking. He told me to watch my step."

"Wow. I didn't see that coming. I knew Alex had a screw loose, but still. Amy, I am so sorry that you are having to deal with all of this. So, he knows you have been digging around. Do you think they are in it together or is Alex acting alone? He knew you were at the restaurant somehow. Do you think he was there watching you?"

"I don't really know. He told me that James is long gone. Either he is watching him too, or they are communicating. My gut is telling me that they have been in on it together from the start now. I am just so confused. I don't know why James agreed to meet me at all. He could have just ignored me. This all seems so elaborate and unnecessary. Not to mention the fact that I just don't want to believe any of it. Alex was there for me after dad died. It's hard to think that it was all fake, you know. Was I just a part of some sick plan? What's the point of any of it? Am I that girl? That dumb, oblivious, easy to manipulate girl?"

"You're right about it all being unnecessary. You aren't that girl, though. You are smart, strong willed, and honestly a bit intimidating. Nothing about you says that you would be easy to manipulate. And no matter what the story is, I don't think you should go home tonight. He has threatened you, with death no less. He could even be watching you. You don't need to be alone. You can stay here tonight. Even if he happened to watch you come here, at least you wouldn't be by yourself if he tried something. I don't have an extra bed, but I will sleep on the couch, and you can have my bed for the night. I will feel much better if I know that you are safe here with me."

"Ok, I will stay here tonight." It would have taken far less to convince me. I had no intentions of being by myself tonight, especially at my house. "But

I will not take your bed. The couch is perfectly fine for me. All I need is a pillow and I will be out like a light."

Xavier did one better and grabbed a set of sheets and some pillows. Before I knew it, I had a lovely place to sleep for the night. And after reassuring him at least ten times that I didn't need anything else, he retired to his bedroom. I collapsed on my comfy new digs.

Now that I was alone with my thoughts, I was beginning to get depressed. Not only had I lost my dad, but I had also now lost a brother and a memory of a wonderful relationship. I didn't even know exactly why either. I needed to know the details, no matter how difficult they would be to uncover. The more I laid on the couch and thought about it, the sadder I became. The void in my chest seemed to be getting bigger. The feeling of despair was crushing.

I wiped the tears that were now flowing from my eyes and quickly stood up. I tried to shake it all off but to no avail. I didn't know what I was doing, but my heart was racing now. I slowly began walking toward Xavier's bedroom. I lifted my hand to knock on the door but changed my mind at the last minute. What if he didn't want me to come in? I couldn't handle any rejection at this point. So without another thought, I reached for the handle and let myself in.

"Amy, is everything okay? Did something happen?" He sat up slightly and squinted at me, but I just shook my head no. I didn't say a word as I closed the door behind me and got closer to him.

"What am I doing?" I kept thinking to myself. I knew what I was doing… I just didn't know what the outcome was going to be. Hopefully I wouldn't wake up in the morning and feel the need to look for another job.

I walked to the edge of his bed, and I pulled back the covers. My heart was pounding but I just went with it. I slid into bed right next to him. Neither of us said a word. I slowly reached my lips for his, hoping he would do the same. The farther I took this, the more humiliating the rejection would be. I could tell that his heart was racing too. His breathing sounded heavier than usual. His movements were a bit awkward.

He grabbed my face with both of his hands and began kissing me back. I was so relieved that he didn't push me away. I needed to be close to someone. We were both filled with so much emotion and loneliness that neither of us could hold anything back. Before I knew it, we were frantically clawing at each other's pajamas; still kissing the entire time.

"Amy are you sure this is what you want?" he asked, stopping briefly. I could tell that he wanted to, so that wasn't the issue. I showed up on his doorstep upset and in tears, and I was vulnerable. He probably felt like he was taking advantage of me by taking things this far. If anything, though, it was probably the other way around.

"Do you not want to?" I could tell that he did, but I still asked.

"I want this more than you know. I just don't want to feel like I am taking advantage of you. I know you are stressed."

"This is exactly what I want." I managed to spout out while trying to catch my breath. And just like that, we were thrown back into the most passionate moment of my life. His kissing moved from my lips down to my neck and collarbone. My hands slowly grazed over his abs, eventually making it down near his waistband and he softly grunted.

"When I said I had never had a girlfriend…" he paused again, not knowing exactly how to say what he wanted to.

"That's alright." I whispered to him as I curled my fingers underneath his pajama pants. I knew he was trying to say that all of this was new to him. It didn't surprise me considering the demanding life he had. He didn't have time for relationships or even flings. I couldn't have cared less.

He tossed me back down on the bed and began

kissing my neck again. I couldn't wipe the smile off of my face as I kissed him back. I ran my fingers through his hair and grabbed a hold of him. I closed my eyes as his kisses began to stray away from my neck. His hand slid up my shirt and my breath hitched. It was all so amazing and surprising at the same time. I never expected by night to end this way and with him. I could feel a fire sparking inside of me.

I sat up so he could take my shirt off and as I laid back down he slid his pajamas off. He laid down beside me, pulling me so close I felt like or bodies might merge together. I wrapped my arms around him as he rolled on top of me. The moment we became one, I could have sworn I saw stars.

It was nothing like I imagined it would be. It was even better. Xavier was passionate and vulnerable. He was everything I loved and hated in a man all rolled into one. And he was beautiful. Even when he was covered in sweat, he still seemed flawless. I hoped that when we were pressed together some of that perfection would stay with me. I got completely lost in the moment.

A year ago, I hated Xavier and everything he stood for. Now that I was here in bed with him, I wanted to be consumed by him. In this moment, he was everything. He was my safety, he was my protector, he was my lover… and I just wanted more.

After it was over, he held me in his arms. I felt so safe and secure as he softly stroked my hair. A part of me hoped that Alex *did* know I was there. I hoped he knew what we were doing. Earlier today I was wishing that I had just moved on. Now, I feel like I really had. During all of my time with Alex, I never experienced anything this incredible.

"Will you stay in here with me tonight? I don't want you to go back to the couch." Xavier asked as he nuzzled his nose into the nape of my neck. I smiled at the request.

"I'm glad that's what you want because I wasn't planning on going anywhere. I feel so safe with you."

"You are safe with me, sweetheart. I won't let anyone get close to you. I promise."

He kissed me on the forehead and snuggled up next to me when I rolled over to my side. I don't think being the little spoon ever felt so wonderful. Knowing that nobody would get to me here, I let myself fall asleep.

CHAPTER ELEVEN

I was confused when I awoke the next morning. Not only was I not in my own bedroom, but I quickly became aware of the arm that was draped over me. Everything came rushing back to me when I opened my eyes to see Xavier laying next to me. He was still asleep. I was instantly giddy as I began mentally replaying the events of last night. He must have sensed that I was awake because he began to stir.

"Good morning beautiful." he rolled over and said to me with a smile.

"Good morning." I said back timidly, as I became aware that I was still naked and very vulnerable. I tucked myself in the blankets. They were so warm and plush. I needed to get some of these for my house.

"I don't think I have ever seen you act this shy before. You aren't regretting anything that happened last night, are you?" He seemed like he was afraid to even ask the question.

"No, not at all. Last night was amazing. I didn't want it to end." I just couldn't stop smiling.

"It doesn't have to completely end, you know. We can pick up right where we left off after work this evening." I knew I should probably say no. He was my boss after all. But just the thought of brushing all of this off left me feeling empty almost instantly. I wasn't ready to let go just yet.

"I think that sounds like a great idea." I said, smiling as I gave in to the warm, gushy feelings I was starting to feel. I hoped that he wasn't playing me.

We both got up and started getting ready for work. I was at a disadvantage since I had not been home since yesterday before dinner. I made do just fine, though. Luckily, I carried spare makeup and a backup change of clothes in my car. We were ready to go at the same time but took separate cars to work. We didn't want anyone at the office gossiping about us. The last thing I needed in my life was gossip and more drama. We didn't even fully know what was going on between us anyway. There was no reason to start idle chatter for a short-lived fling. If it ended up being something more… well, we didn't need anyone interfering with that either. We would cross that bridge when we got to it.

No matter how giddy I was feeling about Xavier right now, I couldn't help but think of James. Were my instincts about him killing my father correct? In the back of my mind, I had been hoping that my theory was wrong. I wanted the three of us to be a family again. I didn't want my mom to find out about any of this either. It would set her so far back. She had made so much progress.

And what part did Alex play in all of this? Was our relationship just a sham? I was so baffled by all of it. I didn't know if trying to get in touch with James was a good idea or not, but I decided to send him a text.

"I hope you are ok. I would really like to talk. Love you, Amy."

Simple and to the point. I wanted to come across more concerned for him than anything else, despite what the truth was. Just as I expected, though, he didn't respond.

When we got to the office Xavier and I went our

separate ways. I was thankful that I had left myself some work yesterday. I needed something to keep me occupied. There was so much I wanted to talk to Xavier about. The press releases sitting on my desk were the only thing that would keep me from pestering him today. I didn't want to act like a lovesick little girl. If I was going back to his house tonight anyway, it could wait until then.

And that brought up a whole other subject I had not contemplated yet. Was it even safe for me to go back to my house? What if Alex was waiting for me there or had set some sort of trap? I would have to go back at some point. I needed clean clothes. Plus, I couldn't keep staying at Xavier's house. That would just end up getting awkward. Nothing like being clingy and around 24/7 to ruin a possible new relationship from the start. I would have to figure something else out.

I still had a lot of friends at the police department. I could always phone in a favor from one of them. An escort would keep me safe at my house, at least long enough to grab some things. I would make that call later. The weekend would be here tomorrow, so I had a couple of days before I needed work clothes. I could stay with Xavier until then.

I started on the press releases. After I was finished with those, I called a friend at the newspaper with a story about a breakthrough Xavier's team had just made in clinical trials for ulcerative colitis. I treated myself to an extra break once I was finished. I propped my feet up on the desk, leaned back in the chair, and closed my eyes. I loved the silence of my office. It was calming. I tried to picture myself somewhere peaceful and serene. I imagined I was on a beach, laying in a hammock. Seagulls were chirping in the air and I could hear the waves crashing on the shore. Now all I needed was a pina colada and my vision would be complete.

There was a knock at my door and I was startled out of my daydream. When I looked up, I saw Xavier at my doorway, looking rather amused.

"I'm not interrupting anything, am I?" he asked with a grin.

"Actually, I was drifting away on a beach. It was warm and I was in a hammock with a cocktail in my hand. I could smell the saltwater and coconut oil. But I guess I don't mind being pulled away from it as long as you are the one doing the pulling." I said with a smile.

He walked in and shut the door behind him. My heart jumped once I saw him turn the lock. He walked over to me, pulled me close, and began kissing me. I could feel his pulse beating wildly as he leaned his body up against mine. It quickly became apparent that he wanted a repeat of the night before. I would have laid him out on my desk if my phone hadn't chirped. I had sent some pretty important text messages today, so I needed to check it. He obliged.

"I think we both know why I didn't make it to dinner. I love you, so please leave it at that. Keep your nose out of things. I promise you that it's for the best." James. I couldn't believe that he finally replied. My heart sank as far down as it possibly could. In the back of my mind, I had been hoping that Alex was bluffing. Now I knew that he wasn't. At least I knew who I needed to go after.

I didn't even have to say anything to Xavier. He knew what the message was about. He put his arm around me as I sank into his chest.

"This sucks." I couldn't manage to come up with anything better to say. I felt crushed. I tried to fight back tears, but it was no use. Why did my heart keep breaking?

"I know it does. Look, let's get out of here. It's early and most of the team is already gone. It will be easier to talk about this at my house. You don't need to stay in your thoughts today."

I agreed with him. Honestly, I think I was just sticking around the office because he was there anyway. I needed his help coming up with an action plan. I shoved my things into my briefcase, grabbed my cell phone, and followed him out of the building.

I was surprised to see that we were the only two people left here at all. Other than the basement-dwelling scientists, of course. They were always here. He gave me a quick kiss on the cheek and hopped in his car. I did the same and followed him back to his house.

CHAPTER TWELVE

Two pina coladas later and I was feeling pretty relaxed. It wasn't as exotic as my daydream had been, but at least Xavier was with me. That made it better. He had given me a t-shirt and a pair of boxers to lounge around in. He had changed into the same thing and we were both sipping our adult beverages on the couch. I was already feeling much better than I did at the office.

"So, I have an idea I want to run by you. As you know, the whole reason behind my father's death was his involvement in your immortality research. I think you should go full steam ahead with what you guys were working on. I don't want him to have died in vain and I know he would want the same thing." Even if nothing else in my world made sense right now, that did. My dad would have wanted the research to continue, and I didn't want James to win.

"I think that is a good idea. It's something that has been on my mind as well. I was so hurt by the loss of him that I couldn't bear to continue with the research we had been doing. It's the right thing to do, though. Your father and I had found a new research location we wanted to move a team to right before he was killed. I purchased the land but just left it abandoned. I could assemble a team to go there and start working. If you'd like, I could take you there this weekend. You can see it before everyone else and let me know what you think about it. The location is pretty secluded. I think it's a pretty ideal spot."

I was so excited that he was on the same page I was. It finally felt like progress was being made. Hopefully he would be on board for the entire plan I had in my head.

"I would also like to recruit a friend of mine to start trying to get dirt on James and Alex. Would it be possible for her to have an office at this new facility as well? She is one of the only people that my dad would confide in. You can trust her. I would trust her with my life. She was always like a sister to me… and a second daughter to dad."

"That is fine with me if you vouch for her. I trust your judgment."

And so it was decided. We would begin to assemble a team first thing Monday morning. We would have to make many trips to transport all of the equipment to the new facility. A moving company could not be trusted with our secrets, so we would have it do it ourselves. A security team would also have to be appointed. I hoped Xavier would spend a decent amount of time there too, seeing as how I was planning to. I would call my friend Kate and give her all of the info about the new job I just gave her.

Kate was the only person that I could think of that my father would have trusted with the job. She knew what he did and she respected it. She had written a few publications for him several years ago and she was always professional and discreet with the information that she was given. Not to mention the fact that she had been my close friend since I was ten years old. We hadn't spoken much over the past few months, but I knew that I could count on her. Plus, she had always been better than me at finding dirt on people. Dirt was what I needed now. I knew that the grimy stories she could dig up would lead me to the ugly truth.

She had only met Alex a few times, but she knew

James very well. Part of growing up with me also involved growing up with him. They were never as close as she and I were, but they were always around each other. I knew that what I had to tell her about James would be a blow to her as well. Regardless, she was the only other person to trust with the details.

For right now though, Xavier had convinced me to let it all go and enjoy our weekend together. So we stayed in our pajamas, ordered a lot of take-out food, and just took pleasure in each other's company. We promised not to talk about anything having to do with death, science, immortality, or my family.

It was the single most special weekend of my life. I felt like we shared something so intimate with each other. We discussed our hopes and dreams, stories from when we were little, and why we were the way we were. We had both been living very lonely lives (only within the past year for me) and for now, we were filling that void for each other.

And finally, after two days of guiltless cuddling and indulgence, it was time for me to go home. Xavier begged me not to go, but I didn't want to overstay my welcome. So I called my dad's old friend Bruce at the police department and asked for a favor. He agreed to follow me home and keep watch overnight for me. I assured Xavier I would be fine and bid farewell to him until the following day.

CHAPTER THIRTEEN

All was quiet when I got to my house. I told Bruce that he could stay outside if he wanted, but he insisted on coming in and checking the place out first. He saw right though my fake protest, I'm sure. I didn't want him to know just how nervous I really was. To my relief, he gave me an all-clear thumbs up. I let out a quick sigh and went inside. Thank God for good friends. I was so afraid that Alex had done something to my house. I locked the door behind me and made a beeline for the couch. I flopped down, hugged one of my favorite fluffy pillows, and closed my eyes.

Normally I would be so comforted to be in my home, but now I just missed Xavier. If you would have told me six months ago that he would have had the kind of impact on my life that he had, I would have called you a liar. Now I simply yearned for his presence. I had found something so calming and safe in his embrace that I now felt so alone in my house. Hopefully he wouldn't leave me feeling like a fool in the end. I had things to do, so I snapped myself out of my doldrums and got up.

I slowly went from room to room looking for signs that someone had been in there. Nothing seemed out of place. I don't know what anyone would have been looking for anyway. I had no secrets. I assumed that both James and Alex knew that if I did have any information, I would be too smart to leave it in writing somewhere. Especially Alex. He spent enough time in this house to know that there would be nothing to find. I'm sure he looked around before. He had been here plenty of times when I wasn't here. So once I had assured myself that I was safe and sound, I headed for the shower.

I almost didn't want to wash the weekend of bliss off of me, but I had to. It felt nice to be in my own shower. Afterward, I threw on some comfy clothes and paced around with a glass of wine. I began to pack an emergency bag to keep in my car. I threw in some extra work clothes along with a few toiletries. Who knows when it would come in handy now that things had become such a mess. I gathered some essential items I couldn't live without - rolodex, identification papers, and a scrapbook of my father's life - and threw it in a bag as well. I had to plan as if I would leave here tomorrow and not be able to come back.

If I had to stay at Xavier's house, or even in my car, I would have what was necessary without feeling the need to come back here for something. I felt as if I were living on the edge of something now. It was scary, but at the same time, I was kind of excited. When I was finally done packing any and everything that I could think of, I placed the bags by my front door and made my way to bed.

I closed my eyes as soon as my head hit the pillow. It felt like heaven. Troubling thoughts soon found me though. All I could see in my head was James. I kept going back and forth from happy memories from when we were kids to various scenarios which involved him killing my father. Was immortality so terrible that he would kill our father over it? How could he bring himself to do such a thing? It made no sense to me. Perhaps I didn't know him as well as I once thought I did.

I looked forward to any progress on moving to our new facility that would be made tomorrow. The faster things got along, the faster I could get some answers that I desperately needed. If I could at least get my office set up and Kate's as well, I would be incredibly happy. I was sure that Xavier would have a team moved in there in no time. For tonight, though, I needed to get some sleep. Even after a relaxing evening, I was still just running on fumes.

I got up and took one last peek out of my window to check on Bruce. He was still out there, sitting in his cruiser. Just the sight of him put me at ease. If he got sleepy or anything, he would make sure someone trustworthy took his place. He kept an eye out for my dad many times. Relieved I was safe in my own home for tonight, I got back in bed and drifted off to sleep.

Please, no dreams tonight. I need some peace. Even good dreams would be too much for me tonight.

CHAPTER FOURTEEN

It was a beautiful day outside and Xavier was all smiles when I pulled into the parking lot the next morning. I was happy to see him too. In fact, I was so distracted at the thought that I almost forgot to grab the bags I had packed the night before. When I said goodbye to Bruce before I left, he offered to come back when I got home from work to stay another night, but I declined. I told him that I would probably just stay at a hotel for a while. It wasn't a lie.

I didn't feel right about continuously putting an officer out by asking him to stay at my house, but I also didn't feel safe staying there without any law enforcement presence. A hotel would be adequately comfortable and still secure. I didn't know how Xavier would feel about it but at this point, we were nothing more than colleagues who were dabbling in the art of intimacy. There was no commitment; therefore he had no real say in how I conducted my life.

"Good morning my dear." Xavier greeted me, along with a kiss on the head. "I am glad to see you made it through the night. I can't tell you how many times I wanted to get up and drive over there to make sure you were ok."

"Bruce did an excellent job making sure I was safe. I looked around and didn't see a sign of anyone being in my house at any point. I think I'm ok."

"So, you will be going back there tonight?"

"I haven't decided yet." I don't know why I lied to him. I suppose I didn't want to sound like I had nowhere to go. I wasn't much of a damsel in distress kind of girl.

Offering no more information as to what my plans consisted of, we walked into the building. We were still careful to not give anything away about our romantic situation, so we entered the conference room individually rather than together. I still took my place next to him at the table, though.

"I have a big announcement to make." Xavier declared, grabbing everyone's attention. "I have decided to move full steam ahead with the immortality research. We will be opening our new facility this week. I will begin assembling the team today. If anyone has any questions or comments regarding the team, please see me after the meeting."

Whispers instantly began picking up across the room. Some people seemed shocked that he was finally pressing on with the research while others were more excited at the thought of it. Finally, a hand went up across the room.

"Who will be running the place, sir?" A man whose name I still had not learned asked.

"I will be running things initially. Martin will be in charge here until I have things up and operational. After that, I will bounce back and forth."

I tried hard not to smile. I was happy and relieved to hear that he would be there. It wasn't just because I liked being around him, either. It would be good to have a confidant there to discuss the big picture with. I wouldn't be delving into all of the details with Kate. I wanted to keep her involvement in the whole immortality scheme of things as superficial as possible. If things went badly, I did not want her to be implicated for anything.

The meeting was fairly boring from that point

on. It was back to any new developments that had been made and setbacks that had come up in the past week. I made a brief statement about what was going on in the press and then we were off to our offices. Xavier agreed to swing by my office after he met with the people who wanted to discuss the new operation. So, I grabbed an empty box to pack my things in and headed to my office.

This was going to be my last day here for a long while. I wanted to set up shop in my new office tomorrow. I honestly could not wait. If I could've moved as soon as the meeting was over I would have. It would be good to wait, though. I would be able to move with Kate if I waited and that was important to me. As long as she took the job, that was. I grabbed my cell and dialed Kate as I was sorting through my things.

She sounded excited to be hearing from me when she answered her phone. We went over the standard how have you been formalities and what is new in your worlds before I got to the point of my call.

"Kate, I have to be honest. This wasn't just a call to catch up. I want to offer you a job. It essentially involves you digging up as much dirt on a few people as you can and investigating a few leads. It pays very well, but I can't discuss any specifics with you until you agree to accept the job. All I can tell you is that you would be paid by Nectar Corp and you would be working with me." I hoped I didn't bombard her with too much information, but I had to get it all out there.

"Wow, that's a lot to take in at once. Amy, you have never led me astray. The fact that you have come to me with this tells me that it probably involves you on a personal level. I have been aching to get away from the company I am working for right now, so what the hell. I'll do it. I have one question, though. Nectar Corp is Xavier Holland's company. I thought that he was your enemy. What gives?"

"I don't know where to even begin. A lot has happened since the last time that we chatted. He isn't the person that I thought he was. I have learned that he was a good friend to dad and he wants to help."

"Good enough for me. You can fill me in on all the details when I see you. When do I start?"

"Tomorrow if you can make it." I hoped she didn't mind being put on the spot.

"I sure can. Screw the whole two-week notice thing. See ya tomorrow, babe."

I was ecstatic. My plan was coming together just as I had hoped it would and I now had two people on my side. I gave Kate the directions to her new office and told her I would meet her there around nine. As I hung up the phone a smile beamed across my face. Hope. I finally had something to feel optimistic about. And as I was having a small mental celebration, Xavier finally came by to see me.

"You look very happy about something." he grinned as he entered my office and closed the door behind him.

"I am. I just got off the phone with Kate. She accepted my job offer and is going to begin working at the new facility with me tomorrow. I couldn't be happier with how this is working out in my favor." I said, the smile still reaching from ear to ear.

"Fantastic. I will be starting tomorrow as well and have already assembled a team. Most of them will be there tomorrow, along with the new security staff. But there is one thing we haven't come up with yet. We need to make a name for the new place. I can't keep calling it the new facility. So start brainstorming and let me know what you come up with."

"I will start thinking about it. In the meantime, would it be ok with you if I left for the day? I don't really have any other work to do. If I stay, I'm just gonna sit on my ass and daydream."

"Sure, you know I don't mind. What are your plans? Where are you staying tonight?"

"I was thinking about getting a hotel room. I just don't feel safe at my house. I packed some things last night and brought them with me."

I could tell by the look on his face that he was hurt I didn't ask to stay with him. He didn't say anything, though. I think he would have felt vulnerable by asking. I had made it this far without depending on someone, I didn't want to start now. The last time I needed someone (Alex) I just ended up getting hurt.

"I will call you when I get settled. Maybe we can have dinner or something." I didn't want to completely shut him out. He was really important to me after all.

"That would be great. If you need anything in the meantime, I'm just a phone call away." He maintained a grin on his way out, but I could feel his disappointment.

I gave him a quick hug before he was completely out of the room and gathered my things. I took one last look around the office I had grown so accustomed to and closed the door behind me. I would miss it here, but Xavier and Kate would be with me at the new place. It would be great.

When I made it to my car, I set my GPS for the nearest Grand Hotel. Just because I was staying in a hotel didn't mean I couldn't allow myself a little luxury. Plus, it was convenient that it was only ten minutes away from Xavier's house. I never knew when I might need a helping hand.

Instead of going out to dinner, I invited Xavier over to the hotel for room service and a movie. Lowkey wasn't a bad idea right now. Plus, this way I could lounge around in comfy clothes.

I was surprised to see a flower bouquet in Xavier's hand when I answered the door.

"I have never seen pajamas look so sexy." He said with a smile as he gently tucked my hair behind my ear.

I just blushed and let him in. If he only knew how much time I spent getting ready, pajamas or not.

We sat on the bed and inspected the room service menu. There were so many tasty options to choose from. Finally, we decided to just order an assortment of dishes to share. Once our order arrived, we put on a movie and got comfy.

"I've had a lovely time with you tonight." Xavier said as the credits rolled.

"It doesn't have to be over yet." I said as I ran my fingers across his chest. The instinctive sound he made, almost like a low growl, excited me.

He pulled me close and, in an instant, everything else in life faded away.

"I can't get enough of you, Amy." he said in between kisses. I smiled as he pulled his shift off. I followed his lead and was lost in passion in an instant.

"I could definitely get used to this." He said as we just laid in bed, sweaty and intertwined.

The truth was, even though the thought of it scared me, I could too.

"You can stay with me if you'd like." I said, hoping he wouldn't say no.

"I was hoping you would say that. Although, you could have saved the money and just stayed at my house. I understand why you didn't, though." He gave me a wink.

"I know, I know. I will stay there for the rest of the weekend."

And that's exactly what I did. Once I finally let go of caring how I would be perceived by Xavier by staying with him, I felt a lot less burdened. Well, that *and* letting go of my need to always be in control. It was the best weekend I had in years.

CHAPTER FIFTEEN

The move to the new facility was going surprisingly well. Kate showed up on time and we were busy turning our offices into something we were proud of. It was girly, professional, and my new home away from home.

Xavier had been in and out. He was busy moving things in, assigning scientists to their new posts, and making plans. I was happy to see that he was making time to see me in the midst of it all. It was nice to feel so loved.

"So, who are we digging up dirt on anyway?" Kate asked, startling me. I had been lost in thought.

I hesitated. I almost forgot that she and I were going to have this chat at some point. I told her what her job was, but not who it was. This should be an interesting conversation.

"James and Alex." I said, so quietly I wasn't sure if she had heard me at first. Did I even speak at all?

"What the hell? Why? What's going on?"

It was hard to tell if she was angry or just shocked. It wasn't an easy subject to approach. I don't know why I expected her to have a better reaction. Surely that was the last thing she was expecting to hear.

"I believe they know something about who killed my dad, but I haven't been able to find anything out. They are hiding something from me. I can't do this on my own. You are the only one I could turn to for help. You are one of the only people outside of the family that my dad even trusted. I know this is like dropping a bomb on you. I'm sorry for that."

She took a minute to think about everything I had just told her. It was a shock. She had been close to James and knew Alex fairly well. I don't think she would have ever guessed that they would have betrayed any of us. She agreed to stay and help me, and we pressed on. Thank God I had her to help me with this.

Kate and I got right to work. She was busy making phone calls and digging up dirt on my suspects, while I was busy putting all of the information she was getting together. I treated each bit of information as if it were a puzzle piece. Unfortunately, the puzzle board was huge and I had no idea where to piece things yet. Little by little, though, things were beginning to add up.

"How are things coming along?" Xavier asked as he popped into the room.

"So far so good. Kate is getting me some good leads. I'm so glad she is part of this team. I also came up with a name for this place."

"Oh you did, huh? Do tell. I have come up with nothing so far."

"Andra. It is Swedish for 'second'." I knew he would like it. His mother was Swedish and I knew that he was very fascinated with his heritage. He didn't have meatballs and hot chocolate laying around his house or anything, but there were a lot of maps and books.

"I absolutely love it. Andra it is. Excellent job, Amy. You never disappoint me." He left our office with a smile on his face.

I must have been smiling like a fool as well

because Kate began to get suspicious.

"What is up with that?" She asked excitedly. "Someone looks smitten."

"What are you talking about?" I knew exactly what she was talking about. I had not said a word to Kate about my involvement with Xavier yet. I guess I didn't have to now. It was probably completely obvious that something was going on between us. I didn't want it to be like that, though.

"I mean, what is going on with the two of you? Are you sleeping together? A couple? In love? Don't lie to me either; I know there is a story there. I know you well enough to know there is something you aren't telling me."

I immediately began to blush. She was right, I couldn't lie.

"I don't know exactly. Sleeping together, yes. A couple, maybe. In love… who the hell knows? This was all very unexpected." It felt like my cheeks were bright red.

"I can't believe you didn't say something to me." She punched me in the arm. "For all I knew, you still thought that he was the one who killed your dad. This brings me to another point. If he isn't the killer… who is? Is that why I am digging up dirt on James and Alex? Amy… your own brother? Is that what he is hiding?"

I didn't know where to start. The fact that I hadn't told her my revelation about Xavier had slipped my mind. I guess the last time we had a heart-to-heart was longer than I thought. So, I started at the beginning. I told her everything, from my first day at Nectar to the day I called and offered her this job. She was one of the few people that my father trusted, so I figured that I could trust her with all of this information.

"Amy, I can't believe you have been keeping all of that in. Next time call me. We have always been close; you know that you can trust me with anything. I love you. You're like a sister to me."

"I know I can. You're like a sister to me too. I guess everything has been happening so quickly that I haven't had a chance to sit down and put it all in words for someone." I breathed a big sigh of relief. She hugged me and we got back to work.

We had talked for so long that the workday was nearly gone once we got back to it. After an hour, I told Kate to go home and get some rest. I would see her back here in the morning. The truth was that I just wanted a shot at some alone time with Xavier. So I decided to stay camped out in my office until he came by. I knew he would check back in.

I didn't have much to do in the way of work since Kate had gone. I just sat there staring at all of the notes we had jotted down, trying to make sense of it all. I still didn't know how Alex fit into all of this. It was all connected somehow. Luckily, I wasn't left alone with my thoughts for very long.

"All alone?" Xavier asked as he strolled in.

He looked like he had a long day. His shirt was un-tucked, his tie pulled loose and his five o'clock shadow was progressing into much more than stubble. I couldn't help but stare a little. If he only knew how sexy he looked. He dropped into Kate's chair and kicked his feet up on the desk.

"Rough day in the labs?"

"Not exactly rough. Just long and seemingly never-ending. We are making progress, though. I didn't expect much with this being the first day, but everyone is working at full speed. I definitely picked the right team."

"That's great. Where are you guys at with the research?"

"I think we have ironed out what should be in the serum. We will be ready to inject it into one of the lab rats tomorrow. We won't see any progression as far as his life span goes, but we should be able to test for strength and agility. If it works, then the rat should be impervious to any disease we inject it with. If not, the rat will die."

"That's amazing. I can't believe how close you are." I didn't expect anything like this for weeks.

"There is still a lot of progress to be made before it can ever be injected into a human, though. God knows what would happen to me if we tested it on a person too soon. They would string me up by my toes. My conscience wouldn't allow it anyway. How was your day? Any good leads?"

"A lot of them, but I still don't know how everything fits together. Maybe after a good night of sleep, it will all be clearer."

"Speaking of sleep, what are your plans tonight? I know you have that hotel room, but I was hoping that you would accept an invitation to sleep at my place."

I hesitated. I knew that I should decline and go to the hotel room I was paying for, but something about the disheveled look he was sporting looked so sexy. I just couldn't resist.

"Why not. Are you leaving soon?" I started getting butterflies in my stomach.

"As soon as you are ready, dear."

Without another word, I stood up and walked toward the door with a smile. He grabbed my hand and led me out of the office.

"I don't care who sees. I am crazy about you and

I'm tired of hiding it. It's not like they will fire me. This is my company."

I didn't protest. I didn't care either. There was so much darkness in my world that I wanted to hold on to the light. So when we got in the parking lot I hopped in his car rather than getting in mine.

"I don't want to hide either. It's all or nothing."

Xavier just smiled as he started the car and left the parking lot.

CHAPTER SIXTEEN

When we arrived at Andra the next day, there were many whispers. We didn't care though. Last night had been one of the best nights of my life. Xavier and I had a romantic dinner followed by the best sex I had ever had. Those stars I thought I saw the first night looked like specks of dust comparatively. It was like being open about our relationship had opened up something inside both of us. As for what our relationship was exactly, we determined that as well. We were a couple. I was looking forward to telling Kate since I didn't have a definitive answer for her last time we spoke.

But Kate wasn't in the office when I got there. All to be found was a post-it note on her computer screen.

"I'm sorry, Amy." That was all the note said. That perfect cursive was unmistakable. It was a note from Kate.

Questions began racing through my mind. What was she sorry for? Was she in danger? I tried to call her cell over and over, but I never got a response. I left a message each time. I told her I wasn't mad. I just wanted to know that she was okay, but I never get a call in return.

After the initial shock set in, fear found its way to me. I had given her so much information about what we were doing. What if she went to the other side? What if that was the side that she had been on all along? There was also the chance that they had gotten to her. Maybe they found out what we were doing, and they took her for information. I didn't know what to do. What had I done?

I took off in a sprint toward the labs. I made it to the door and rang the bell. I couldn't barge in if they were doing any kind of testing. A scientist I didn't know came to the door and I asked if he could send Xavier out.

"What's wrong? Are you okay?"

I was sitting on the floor in a panic when Xavier came out of the lab. I didn't mean to scare him but I was freaking out.

"Kate's gone. All that was in our office this morning was a note that said she was sorry. I've tried calling her, but she doesn't answer or call me back. I don't know what to do. I'm sorry for bothering you but I didn't know who else to go to. Xavier, she knows so much. What have I done?" I was covered in tears at this point.

"You aren't bothering me. We will figure this out. They can keep working without me for a little while. I'll go back to your office with you."

Xavier put his arm around me and walked me back to my office. I cried the whole way. He sat me down in my chair once we got to my office and got down on his knees in front of me. He wiped the tears from my face and held my hand.

"I know you are scared and upset, but I promise you we will figure this out. It's going to be okay."

But unfortunately, we got nowhere. Kate never called back. We couldn't go to the police without having to tell them the whole story. We knew it would be too much trouble. There would be so many questions that we just couldn't answer. So for now, we planned to hope for the best but prepare for the worst.

Xavier eventually went back to the lab and I was left alone in my office with my thoughts. I kept going over all of the years I spent with Kate. I had always been better friends with her than James, but had that changed in recent years?

What about Julie? We were all friends. Had she stabbed me in the back too? I pulled out my phone and called her.

"Hey Banana!" she sounded chipper. Also, I hadn't heard anyone call me that in years. I was surprised she remembered that nickname.

"Hey, Jules. Listen, I'm at work right now, but I've run into some issues. Have you talked to Kate recently?"

"I've tried, but she always sends me to voicemail and never returns my calls. Last time I saw her was about a year or so ago right before she moved. I bought her a housewarming gift and she never even thanked me. What a biatch! Why do you ask anyway? She giving you the cold shoulder too?"

"I don't know. I think she just stabbed me in the back in a pretty big way."

"That doesn't surprise me. You know she always had the hots for Alex."

What? I was taken back. Her feelings for Alex were not something I ever knew about. This was all making me feel nauseous. And stupid.

"Look, I gotta go. I'll call you back tonight, okay?"

"Alright girl, hang in there. Don't stress about Kate. If she doesn't want to act like a friend to us anymore, then she's not worth our time or thoughts. You know where to find me."

I let out a sigh of relief when I hung up. At least not everyone had turned again me. I wish I could've told Julie the whole story. A it stood, I had told far too many people.

I needed to try to let this all go for now and do some work. I probably wouldn't be able to do it easily, but I had to try.

I did what I could to keep myself busy. I was tracking down leads to the best of my ability, given my current state. I made myself a timeline of James's life… the best I knew of it at least. I pinpointed the time that I became aware of his and Alex's friendship. There had to be some significance there. I grabbed my notebook of dad's accomplishments to reference with the timeline.

There it was. James and Alex's friendship lined up with the time that my father was interviewed about the rumors of his involvement in cloning sheep. My father denied that he had any part in the research, but James never believed him. Alex didn't badmouth my father, but he did speak out against the others involved. It would make sense that this was the time that they met.

Was it possible that it had been a scam the whole time? Was my relationship with Alex just a part of their plan? Maybe he got close to me so that I wouldn't suspect him and James of this crime. I felt so dirty and used. I cringed at the thought. There wasn't much to question… the evidence was staring me in the face. Looking back on it now, I don't know how I could be so naïve. Perhaps I was just so desperate to find someone to fill the void that my father had left that I was willing to overlook the truth. Not anymore. I would expose those two for what they were, no matter what it took.

The discovery ignited something inside of me. I began placing calls and taking notes like there was a ticking time bomb that I was trying to beat. I figured it all out. When James and Alex met, when they began planning the murder and how they dumped the body without anyone knowing. The only thing I had yet to uncover, though, was their current location. Now I had a new plan I had to forge. Serving life in prison was no justice in my eyes. They needed to die. As soon as I was able to track them down, I could put a plan in motion to rid the world of them.

So for now, my new focus would be what to do when I found them. Xavier would hate the idea, but

I wanted to be the one to end their lives. I would have to get a gun that couldn't be traced back to me. I would need a way to lure them away from each other. I didn't know for certain that they were together, but it made sense to me that they would be. They were all each other had at this point and they would need to stick together if they had any hope of surviving. I hoped that was the case at least.

I spent the next eight hours plotting. I was a perfectionist already and this plan had to be immaculate. There would be no room for deviation. I would have to be quiet and quick. If they sensed my presence at all, I was certain that they would jump ship and my chance would be lost. The only question in my mind right now was Kate. I wished I knew which team she was on. Hope for the best and prepare for the worst… I had to plan as if she was on team evil as well. Only God knew how much I hoped that wouldn't be the case. I think I would feel more betrayed by her than I felt by James, and he was my brother.

I was glad I hadn't seen Xavier for the rest of the day. I needed to be in solitude to hatch my plan. Something about that man brought out my vulnerable side. That was the last thing I needed getting in the way right now. Still, I knew that I would have to tell him what my plan was. I didn't want him to be a part of it though. I knew how much he loved my father and he would want to avenge him. Whatever feelings he had for me would play a part in that too. I couldn't bear risking his reputation. He had worked so hard and sacrificed so much, I wouldn't let him throw it all away for me.

Still, I knew I would have to let him in on what I had been doing all day before I left. So, I sent him a text message asking him to stop by my office whenever he had a chance. I wasn't at all surprised when he replied less than a minute later saying he was on his way. So I straightened up my paperwork and sat patiently until he arrived.

"Hey, babe. Sorry I haven't checked in all day. We have had some great breakthroughs! The rat has been impervious to every single disease we have injected it with. He is faster and stronger. It has been such an amazing day. How have things been going over here? Any better?"

"I have had many breakthroughs as well. I have pinpointed when, I think, James and Alex became acquainted. I have figured out the entire timeline of events as well. The only thing I haven't been able to determine is what their current location is."

"Wow Amy, that is great. What do you plan to do with this information?"

"Well, that's the thing. I don't think you are going to like where I am going with this. I am hoping to find their location… at which point I plan to kill them." It sounded a little different than I expected once I said it out loud. Honestly, it sounded silly.

"Um, kill them or have them killed?"

"I want to do it myself. They took away such a big part of my life and I want to be the one that ends theirs. This should be on my hands, not someone else's."

Xavier just stood there staring at me, almost in disbelief. It was the first time that I had ever seen him speechless. It made me nervous.

"I know what you are thinking. You think I am crazy. I am not going to argue with you on that point because I very well may be. You and I both know that we can't go to the cops about any of this. Can you imagine what would happen if they knew what we were doing here? I mean, you are trying to make people immortal. That would not go over well at all. I just think this is the only way for justice to be served. Not to mention how much better it will make me feel. I can't just let this go, Xavier."

Xavier sat down in Kate's chair and let out a big sigh. I was so nervous. I didn't know what he would say. The look on his face told me enough about what his thoughts were on the subject.

"I'm not going to argue with you either. In the back of my mind, I already knew that it was going to come to this eventually. I just don't want you to do it by yourself, Amy. These guys are dangerous. We don't know what they are capable of. You don't need to be in that situation alone."

"Well, what about the immortality serum?"

"What about it?"

"Inject me. If I were immortal then they wouldn't be able to do anything to me. I would be unstoppable."

"You don't know what you are asking!" I couldn't instantly tell that he was angry. "This serum isn't just something you can play around with. We don't know how it fully works yet. Those rats could die tomorrow because of something we haven't thought of. That's why we run so many tests. That's not to mention what it means in the grand scheme of things. It means that you can never age. You can never die. You will watch everyone you care about die and you won't even be able to be there with them because they would have too many questions about why you still look like you are in your twenties. Don't let your desire for revenge cloud your judgment."

I didn't even know what to say to that. I felt like anything that came out of my mouth would just anger him further. I know he didn't think I was taking his work seriously, but I had thought of the risks. Maybe not to the extent that he just mentioned, but I had given it thought. For me, it would be worth it. It was not worth a fight, though. Not right now, at least.

"I'm sorry. I didn't mean to make this all seem less serious than it is." I didn't know what else to say.

"I didn't mean to fly off the handle. I just care about you. I want to keep you safe and I don't know how safe my answer for eternal life is yet. There is so much more to it that you haven't considered. We will figure something out, I promise."

I didn't tell him that I was going to do this on my own. He would never be okay with it. He would probably hire someone to follow me around and I couldn't risk that. For now, I excused myself from the office and told him I was gonna head back to my hotel and get some rest. He didn't try to protest my desire to go to the hotel and I was thankful. There was nothing more I needed right now than some time alone.

I grabbed all of the notes I had taken throughout the day. I didn't want anyone stumbling upon any of it. I gave Xavier a hug and kiss goodbye and sped away from the building. I had never felt as burdened in my life as I did right now. It was as if I had a 100-pound weight on my back and I couldn't escape from its pressure no matter what I tried. The only way to get rid of it was to kill those responsible for it.

I made it to the hotel in record time. I was

thankful that there had been no cops around because I would have gotten a ticket for sure. I gathered my things and went inside my room.

This was no luxury hotel, but it was good enough. The bed was comfortable and there the bathroom had a garden tub, which I was headed to almost immediately. I filled it with the hottest water I could stand and a little bubble bath. I slipped in and closed my eyes in an effort to relax my troubles away. It didn't work completely, but it did make me more relaxed. I tried to focus on the task at hand. Where were they?

The last time I spoke to James, he was in town. There was no doubt that he was gone long before I made it to the restaurant. I tried to think of any of the places I had heard him mention before. Vacation spots or places he had been to on business. Was there a place he visited more often than any others?

It hit me like a ton of bricks… Alabama. He always said he loved the south. It was easy to disappear down there he once told me. I focused hard on remembering a time when Alex had mentioned the same location, but I couldn't think of one. As far as I could remember, Alex never mentioned being anywhere other than here. I would go with the assumption that he would go wherever James told him to go. I had never been anywhere south, other than a trip to Disney World when I was about six. If they were to hide there, they would definitely have the advantage of knowing their way around. I would be running blind. The more I thought about it, the more certain I became that Alabama was where I could find them. It wasn't a small state though. It was rural and spread out. How would I find them there?

My immediate instinct was to call Xavier and share the news I had come up with, but I stopped myself. If I was going to tell him any of this, I needed to have my facts straight first. For now, I would say nothing about my discovery until he asked me specifically about it. He would probably ask me in the morning when I got to the office, but I would cross that bridge then. For now, I would soak until all of the bubbles were gone.

CHAPTER SEVENTEEN

From the second my eyes were open the next morning, my mind was racing. I had such big hopes for the day. Now that I thought I knew where I could find Alex and James, I needed to put my plan together. I hoped that Xavier would be so busy in the lab that he wouldn't have much time for me. I felt a bit guilty for feeling that way, but I couldn't help it. I did like him a lot and I was still happy that we were a couple, but right now he was not my top priority. As much as I didn't want to, I forced myself to get up and out of bed. I didn't want to start planning here, just to get up and go to work in the midst of all of it.

I rushed around the hotel room trying to get ready. The faster I got to work, the faster I could be on my way to killing these bastards. I somehow managed to brush my teeth and my hair at the same time. Not bad for determination. I threw on an outfit and I was out the door. My makeup was minimal, but I didn't even care. On any normal day, I would have taken the extra time to look nice, especially now that Xavier and I were seeing each other. After all, I'm in my early twenties and allowed to still have a bit of teenage vanity about me. Today I couldn't care less.

I pulled into the parking lot and rushed inside to my office. I was happy to see a cup of coffee sitting on my desk, considering I was rushing around too quickly to remember to stop and get a cup. There was no sign of Xavier, who was the only one that would have left the cup, but just a note with a heart on it. I smiled. He must have gotten to work early this morning. I wasn't going to bother him. I opened my notebook and began to jot things down.

So what did I know so far? Not much, but hopefully my assumption that they were in Alabama was correct. The only city I ever remember him talking about was a place called Everville. Or was it Evergreen? I looked it up online. It was Evergreen. From what I could tell, it seemed like a good place to hide. Very rural… a small town. The population was close to 3,000. I'm sure people kept to themselves there. On the other hand, that could mean that locals would be quick to notice an outsider. Perhaps they would stand out without even realizing it.

For now, I would plan on that being where I could find them. I looked for cities close enough for me to stay, but far away enough for them not to notice me. Montgomery seemed like my best bet. The city was bigger, with about 100,000 residents or so. I would blend in more. Not to mention there would be more places to stay.

I would have to travel under a name different than my own. That would rule any air travel out of the equation. Security had gotten so strict after September 11th, that there would be no hope of me getting away with using a fake name. The last thing I needed was to be arrested because they thought I was a terrorist or something. So, I would have to find a car to drive and get a fake ID as well. Once I got there and was settled in I could start recon. I made a quick mental note to pick up a pair of cowboy boots. Surely that would help me blend in. Hopefully it didn't make me look like a poser.

One of my old journalism colleagues did a piece on how easy it was to change your identity. I was shocked at some of the information they uncovered during their research. He would be able to point me in the right direction.

The real challenge would be to find them once I was there. I needed to make a list of the types of places they may frequent. Any bar in town would be a given for James. Alex took good care of himself and was a bit of a heath nut, so I listed local gyms and farmers' markets for him. They would probably have enough money saved up so they wouldn't have to depend on any type of odd job, so I could rule that out. Other than that, they would probably lay low. I would have to stick to the shadows while I was down there.

After I found James and Alex and studied their routines, I would need to begin scouting out locations to eradicate them. The ideal place would be wooded. It would need to be secluded, but also in a loud enough area that no one would notice any sounds they made. It should be easy to find a wooded place around Evergreen. As of now, I didn't know how I would kill them, other than slowly. If the area I found was isolated enough, I would probably bury the bodies there. I didn't want to risk driving around with bodies in my car. How risky would it be to leave them there, though?

It was hard to believe that I was sitting here, coming up with such a plan. Had life really taken me to this point? Could I be this person? There was no other option. Unfortunately.

I couldn't leave just yet. I wanted to give them

more time in Alabama. They needed to feel like they were safe. The safer they felt, the less cautious they would act. That would hopefully give me the opportunity I would need to take them out. Plus, there were still a lot of loose ends I would need to tie up around here before I flew the coup. I would also need an alibi if I was going to keep Xavier in the dark about what I was doing. He would be right behind me on my way to Alabama if I told him my plan.

I would wait until next Friday to do anything. That would give them more time to relax down south and give me more time to sort everything out.

CHAPTER EIGHTEEN

Friday got here before I knew it. I had been so busy finalizing my plan that time flew by. Xavier was fully occupied as well. Their immortality research had been going better than expected. He could barely tear himself away from the lab long enough to get a few hours of sleep each night. He had even set up a cot in one of the offices for those nights when he didn't want to drive home at all.

Don't get me wrong, we had found time for each other. We were both busy, though and that kept him from asking too many questions. I hated lying to him and that helped. I told him I had been busy trying to track down leads about how James and Alex met and any projects they had worked on together in the past. That was all true. I was doing that research and it was paying off. I learned of a few ventures the two of them had together that I didn't know about. It showed me how dark they truly were.

Today was the last day I was planning on being in town. I didn't want to lie to Xavier about it, so I decided that I would tell him. I was going to take the coward's way out, though. I was planning on coming into the lab later tonight after he should be gone to leave him a note about it. I would tell him I was going south, but I wasn't getting more specific than that. Hopefully, he wouldn't be at the lab when I came back in to leave the note. It was easy to leave an important message in a note, but it is quite harder to say the message to someone's face. There was no way I could look him in the eyes and lie.

I sat at my desk quietly contemplating the right wording for the note I was going to leave when Xavier walked in.

"What do you look so happy for?" I asked, unable to ignore the smile on his face.

"I think today is the day that we will know whether or not this serum is the real deal. We are on the brink of a breakthrough, and I am staying all night until we get it."

I tried not to let my disappointment show. I was happy that he was so close to success, but I was worried that he would catch me when I came in tonight. I would try my best to keep quiet. Hopefully, he would be so busy in the lab that he would never even know that I was there. For now, though, I would do what I could to cherish the last bit of time we had together. There was always the chance that I would not make it home from Alabama. If I were to not make it back, I wanted his memories of me to be sweet, not those of betrayal.

"I know you are very busy, but how long of a break were you planning on taking?" I asked, hoping he could devote a small amount of time to me.

"I had no set time in my brain. Why do you ask? Have something in mind?"

"I thought it would be nice to have lunch together. Do you have enough time to leave and grab a bite to eat with me?"

"I will always have time for you, my dear." he said with that smile I had grown to be so fond of.

He took off his lab coat and threw it on my chair as I grabbed my purse. We left Andra hand in hand on the way to lunch. We decided to stick to somewhere close to the lab. While he did have the time for me, he still had a schedule to keep up with.

We settled on Time's Diner. It was a small place, but we liked it. It had more of a mom-and-pop feel as opposed to another chain restaurant. There weren't any tacky decorations on the walls, just pictures taken at various times throughout the town. The food selections on the menu were original and it all tasted amazing, like it was made with love.

I ordered the "down-home chicken sandwich" and Xavier had the meatloaf. It was nice to spend some time together outside of the office.

"We have been so busy lately, it's nice to get out with you." he said taking my hand in his.

"I think so too. It's hard to remember the last time we saw the light of day together. We need to make more time to do this."

"Well, if today has the results I expect it to, then we will have more time. I will be happy when all is said and done so I can get out of that lab. As much as I love my work, it sucks not having any personal time. I just want to take a walk or sit at home and watch a movie, you know?"

"Yeah, I know what you mean. I have been so preoccupied lately that I haven't done anything for myself. I'd love to go get a massage and a manicure."

Our food came to the table and we stopped talking. I think that we had both been living on basic sandwiches and chips lately. It was so amazing to be eating real food that neither of us could carry on a conversation while doing so. When we finished eating, we both laughed.

"I didn't realize how good that would be. You must have felt the same because I don't think either of us said a word once the plates hit the table." Xavier said, still laughing.

"Oh my gosh, I forgot how good real food was." I giggled as I put my napkin on top of my plate.

Xavier paid the bill and we slowly walked out to the parking lot, both of us bursting at the seams. We moaned as we got into the car and buckled up. We sat quietly through the drive back to work. Comfortable silence. It was something I had grown to enjoy.

"I don't know how I am going to get any work done now. I just want to curl up on that cot and take a nap." Xavier said as we pulled up to Andra.

"Me too. I am so full. That was nice, though. Thanks for lunch babe."

"Don't mention it." he said to me as he kissed the top of my head.

He gave me one last hug before we went our separate ways. It was hard to let go. I wanted to tell him what I was up to. I wanted to ask him to come with me and I knew he would. But instead, I swallowed my cowardice and said I would see him later.

I didn't plan to spend much more time at the office. I needed to go back to my hotel and prepare for my trip. I still had to shower and pack up all of my things. It would be smart to leave a note in my room detailing where I was in case things went badly. I was sure that Xavier would think of going there if I didn't come home. So, for now, I finalized all of the details of my plan and waited for two more hours to pass so that I could leave.

I didn't say goodbye to Xavier when I left the office. I was too much of a coward. Hopefully, I didn't regret it. I knew I would give in and tell him everything if I saw him again. So, I just grabbed my things and left.

CHAPTER NINETEEN

I wiped the steam off of the mirror in the bathroom of my hotel room when I got out of the shower. I stared back at myself. The stress of this year had aged me and it made me angry. I would add that to the emotions that were driving me down south. I dried my hair and gathered all of the items I had scattered around the bathroom. I threw them in a bag and began doing the same with the rest of my belongings. After everything was packed up, I sat down to write a note to Xavier.

If you are reading this, then my plan did not go off without a hitch. I am sorry that I didn't tell you what I was doing. I knew that if I told you where I was going and why, you would follow me. I couldn't let you risk your life for me. I just couldn't live in a world where James and Alex were free to live out their lives. I needed to see to it that they pay for what they did. I am writing this letter in case I do not make it home.

I figured out that the two of them had to be hiding in Alabama. Evergreen to be exact. So, I am traveling there to hunt them down. I will not leave until they are dead. If I don't make it home, I trust that you will avenge me. I just want you to know that I have cherished our time together. I am truly happy that I got to know you. Thank you for everything you have given me. I love you, Xavier. I really do.

I put the letter on the table next to the bed. I grabbed my bags and headed to the car. Once everything was loaded, I got in and drove to Andra. There was a faint smell of smoke in the air. It was nice weather, so I assumed it was a campfire. But I was horrified to see that it was no campfire when I got to Andra. The whole place was up in flames.

I parked my car on the side of the road and ran toward the building. Tears began to stream down my face at the thought of Xavier still being inside. When I got to the parking lot, though, I didn't see his car. I was relieved, but I could still hear screams coming from inside. There were still scientists in there. I didn't know if I could save them, but I had to try.

Alex. I was almost at the front door when he appeared in front of me.

"You just don't stop, do you Amy?"

"Alex, what have you done? What kind of monster are you?" I cried as I stood before him.

"I'm the kind of monster that was prepared to let you go, but you just kept digging. Found out where James and I were hiding, did you? Yeah, I read the letter you left in your hotel room. You should have known that if your house wasn't safe, a hotel room wouldn't be either. I can find you wherever you go."

I knew that I couldn't reason with him no matter what I said. So, I ran for it. I made it to the side of the building when I heard a single gunshot. My heart jumped and I could feel myself turn pale as I turned to see Alex lying on the ground in a pool of blood.

"You really should have kept your nose out of things, Amy."

James walked toward me, and my heart fell to the floor. He was disheveled and sweaty. His faced was streaked with black from what I guessed was dirt or soot… maybe a bit of both.

"How could you kill him?"

"He was about to kill you, Amy. I couldn't let that happen."

"I don't give a shit about Alex. I was talking about dad. How could you kill our father you son of a bitch?" I screamed with tears pouring down my face. I had thought about what I would say to him when I finally confronted him, but all of those thoughts were long gone now.

"He had to be stopped, Amy. When he came to my house to tell me about this whole immortality nonsense, I tried to reason with him. I tried so hard, Amy. I swear I tried. I didn't want it to come to this, but he wouldn't listen. I couldn't let him go through with it and killing him was the only way to stop him. I thought that it was all over with until Kate told me what you and Xavier were doing here. Now everyone inside will die because of *you*. You are next on the list and then I am going to hunt down your little boyfriend. This is all his fault anyway. Dad would be alive today if it weren't for him and his sick experiments."

There was no time for hesitation. I ran.

I ran as fast as I could through the woods. It was just like in the dream I had. How could that be? I dodged tree branches and hopped over logs, making my way to the river. In my dream, I had stashed aside a raft. In reality, I had not. I didn't know fully what I would do when I made it to the water, but it had to be safer than anywhere near James. If he had killed our father, he would have no problems with killing me. He said he would.

I couldn't believe Kate betrayed me. She had always been such a great confidant to father and me. If I survived this night, she would be at the top of my list. I could hear his footsteps in the woods behind me, but I couldn't stop to see how close he was. Twigs snapped under his feet and each step made me more anxious. I was almost at the water now. When I made it there, I held my breath and jumped in. I had no other choice. The current was strong and the water began tossing me around like a rag doll. I could hear gunshots behind me. James must have decided not to jump in and try to shoot me instead. I kept praying that he would miss me. He emptied the clip and I thought that it was over. I almost smiled I was so relieved. He must have had another clip on the ready because I heard another shot and was instantly in pain. That one didn't miss.

The water got calmer the further downstream I made it. I did my best to swim to get further faster, but it was hard with a bullet wound in my shoulder. The pain was excruciating. It was hard to tell how much blood I was losing, but I could feel myself getting weaker by the minute. I needed to make it to land and then to Xavier somehow. I had to get to him before James did. I hoped that my wound would hold up until then.

I made it as far as I could in the water and

crawled onto the land once I got to an embankment. I stood up and began to run once I got my footing. I was losing a lot of blood from the looks of my shirt. I tried to push the thought out of my head as I made my way to Xavier. If he didn't know what was going on, he would probably be at his house. If he did know, I wasn't sure where he would be hiding.

I stuck to the shadows on my way there. If James were out looking for me, I didn't think I could fight him off in the state that I was currently in. The more blood I lost, the less aware I became. My vision was slowly starting to become impaired. It became imperative for me to hurry. And hurry I did, the rest of the way to his house. Thank God I was close.

I saw his car in the driveway once I got there and was more than mildly relieved. I tried to open the front door, but it was locked. I kept hitting the doorbell, hoping he would hurry to the door. I was losing track of how many times I had rung the bell. I leaned up against the door frame and just held my finger down. My peripheral vision was completely black, almost like tunnel vision. Xavier had an expression of horror on his face once he opened the door and saw me. The only word I could squeeze out was "James." That was the last thing I remember before I fell toward him and everything else went black.

CHAPTER TWENTY

I began having the craziest dreams of my life. Most of them were about James. He had dark eyes and a cold stare. He was a monster. At the end of every dream, he killed me. Each time, it was as painful as that gun shot. I used to think that you couldn't die in your dreams. I thought that meant you would die in real life. Each time the dream ended and I didn't wake up, it seemed like that had been an accurate assumption. The conscious part of my brain kept wondering if death was the reason that I wasn't waking up. The longer I dreamt, the more vivid they became. Every detail became more vibrant. The smells became more pungent, the feelings more intense.

Suddenly, everything faded to black and it felt like I was falling. I turned my head side to side, but I couldn't see anything. I held my hand out in front of me, but no matter how fast I waved it in front of my face, I couldn't see it either. Nothingness surrounded me fully. It felt like I began picking up speed and what had started as a slow fall became a swift plunge toward whatever was below me. I was falling so fast I could feel the wind whipping up all around me. I was filled with intense fear, but also an extreme sense of joy. The emotions were stronger than anything I had ever felt before.

Just as I felt that I was going to make contact with whatever I was plunging toward, I felt a hand reach for me and pull me out. Instantly, I was awake. Xavier was by my side when I opened my eyes.

"What happened?" I asked, trying to look around me. My heart was racing. Not only was I confused, but the feeling I had just felt before I woke up was so intense and... different. It appeared I was in Xavier's house. I vaguely remembered making it here... did I fall when I got here? Maybe I bumped my head. That could explain the wild dreams. I couldn't remember why I was coming here, though.

"James shot you. It was really bad, Amy. You lost a lot of blood by the time you made it here. I don't know what kind of gun he had, but your shoulder was very bad. Almost mangled. I don't know how you managed to make it here to me. You have been out of it for days." I had never heard him talk so fast before. He seemed so hyped up. His eyes were bloodshot.

I didn't remember any of what he mentioned happening. I remember running from James and getting to the woods, but everything was sort of blank after that.

"What about James? Why am I not at the hospital? My shoulder doesn't hurt."

"He and Kate took off. I hired someone to find them. So far they haven't turned up. Nobody tries to kill the love of my life and gets away with it." He paused for a moment, as if he were searching for the right words to say. "There is something else I need to tell you, Amy."

I could tell he was serious, so I tried to sit up and give him my undivided attention. Normally I would have cracked a joke about him having a secret family or something. Now wasn't the time for that, though. I was still a bit foggy and confused. At least I wasn't as weak as I would have expected after being shot.

"You lost so much blood. I don't know how you

even managed to make it here. The doctor didn't think you were going to live. Your vitals kept dropping and you were becoming less responsive with each passing minute. You were literally seconds away from death and I had to do something to save you." He began to cry. "So, I injected you with the serum."

He said the last part so quietly, I could barely hear what he was saying.

"The immortality serum? What?" I was lost for words. I didn't know what else to say. What did that mean? Obviously I knew what immortality meant, but what were the ramifications?

"Yes, the immortality serum. I know the consequences of what I have done are everlasting, but I couldn't lose you. Please understand and forgive me. I love you, Amy. My world is nothing without you in it. I'm sorry if I made the wrong choice. I didn't know what else to do."

I sat quietly for several minutes, thinking about what I had just been told. It was a lot to take in. I was immortal. I couldn't die. And from what Xavier had told me about the serum in the past, I should now be super strong, quick, and unstoppable. It was like I fell asleep and woke up as a superhero. Had they been able to finish the research before Andra went down in flames? What if it failed? Was I going to become some kind of mutant?

"Was the serum finished? Did you do anything you needed to before James and Alex torched the place?"

"I had just gotten home when they showed up at Andra. The serum was a success, so I brought a few vials home with me to put in my safe. I never dreamed I would have to use them. But when you showed up here in the state you were in, I had one in hand just in case. I called the doctor over to my house. They would ask too many questions in a hospital. I paid him off to be silent about anything he heard or saw. I knew he couldn't save you in the end, he tried everything he could think of. So, I had to."

I swallowed hard. I was completely stunned. The last thing I remembered was running from James. I didn't remember being injected with anything. That must be why my dreams had become so vivid. They were becoming more intense as my body was changing. I was so overcome with emotions that I began to cry.

My mind kept going over the conversation I had with Xavier when I asked him to make me immortal. I would see all of my friends and family die while I stayed silently in the background. Efforts would have to be made to ensure people didn't catch on that I wasn't aging. I didn't want to live forever if I had to be alone.

"I am so sorry Amy. You think I made the wrong choice. I can see it in your eyes." Xavier looked truly sorrowful. I could see in his eyes that he was beginning to panic.

I couldn't blame him for the choice he made. I would have done the same for him without another thought.

"You didn't make the wrong choice." I said as I wiped the tears from my cheeks. "Thank you for saving me. We will figure all of this out."

I hugged Xavier. For the first time in a while, I felt safe. The feeling of his arms around me made me feel untouchable.

"But what about you Xavier? Can you be immortal with me?" I asked, pulling back to look into his eyes.

Xavier paused for a moment as if he didn't want to tell me what he was thinking. His eyes motioned toward the floor.

"The serum only works if you are dying. If I had injected you while you were perfectly healthy, your immune system would have fought it off. Your body clings to the life that the serum brings only when it is almost gone. I would have to be on death's door for it to work."

The sad look on my face must have said it all. I wanted him with me. I didn't want to be the only immortal. How could I share all of the new experiences I would have with him if he couldn't fully understand how it felt?

"We will figure something out, Amy. I won't stop working until I do. I know you are afraid of walking the earth alone, but you won't. I'm not going anywhere any time soon and I will find the answer to this before that time comes for me. Trust me; there is nothing I want more than to spend eternity with you."

I did my best to smile and reassure him that I believed in him. It wasn't a lie. He was a brilliant scientist and I knew he could figure it all out. It just wouldn't be soon enough. I wanted it to happen now. Knowing there was nothing I could do about it now; I grabbed his hand and led him to the door.

"Let's go for a walk or something. I want to see how different things are for me now." I wasn't completely sure of myself, but if I was immortal now, a little wooziness wasn't going to get the best of me. Not to mention, after the news I just got I definitely needed some air. The room was suddenly feeling a bit small and my claustrophobia was in full affect.

"Great idea, but are you sure you are up for it?" I nodded and opened the door. He followed me outside and we began walking down the block toward the park. It was a beautiful day outside. The wind was blowing and you could smell summer in the air. The difference in my world was instant. It was like I was looking at it all through an amazing pair of glasses. The colors were more vibrant and I could see the tiniest detail in everything. I could smell so much more than usual. I could smell people, food and even flowers from miles away. It was breathtaking.

"Well, how is it?" Xavier asked excitedly. I could tell he couldn't wait to have some real feedback on what he had created. He couldn't help it. It was the scientist in him. There is, after all, only so much that a lab rat can show you.

"It is amazing. Everything is amplified so much. My world is more vibrant and beautiful than ever before. I wish you could see it through my eyes. I didn't know that some of these colors even existed. It is like I am seeing in color for the first time after living in black and white."

"I will someday. For now, I will just have to live it through your words."

We strolled hand in hand for miles down the street. We walked so far that we had made it to the river. The last time I was there was when I was trying to get away from James. And I remembered for the first time since I woke up that I had been shot. I remembered everything.

"My gunshot wound… I can't even see a scar." I peeled back my shirt to take a look.

"That is the amazing thing about immortality. You will never see any scars. Your body regenerates at such a high rate of speed. You should have seen it heal. It was unlike anything I had ever seen before. As soon as I injected you with the serum, it began to disappear… I could see the tendons and muscles reconnecting."

"James didn't come find you? He said he was going to kill me and you would be next."

"Perhaps he thought things would be to hot by the time he could make it to my house. I heard sirens when I opened the door to let you in. The people I have hired haven't seen any trace of him."

That was all a relief to hear. Maybe we would have a bit of a reprieve before there was any more drama. Since I was no longer injured, I decided to hop in the water and swim around a bit. I felt more impulsive than usual.

"What are you doing in there? You still have all of your clothe on." Xavier asked with a big, surprised chuckle.

"I just had to see what it felt like! If colors were more intense, I knew sensations had to be."

"We are going to have to work on your impulse control a bit, I see. Well? How is it?"

"It is exhilarating! I could stay in here for days. I can feel the vibration of the current against my skin. It's like getting a water massage. This is wild."

He just shook his head in laughter as he tried to help me out of the water. I was going to try to pull him in with me, but something stopped me. I could sense something. I suddenly smelled such a distinct smell that I stopped immediately. It smelled like sweat and dirt. It smelled like danger. Why did I think that? Emotions didn't have smells.

"Something is wrong." I said to Xavier, so panicked that I didn't know what else to say.

"What do you mean? What is wrong?"

"I smell something. I can't quite explain it, but I feel like we are in danger. We need to get ho-."

I didn't even have time to finish my sentence before he appeared.

"James. What the hell are you doing here?" Xavier said loudly.

I turned my head and saw James standing on the other side of the river. I gasped.

"I'm here to finish what I started Professor X. You and your little science experiment have got to go. This has gone on long enough. I may have missed the mark last time, but I won't now."

I flew out of the water in one swift move. I was faster than before too. Xavier and I needed to make a run for it. We were in no position to fight right now. We had made it about three steps in the right direction when I saw Kate standing there. She was bruised and slightly bloody, as if she had been beaten up and did a horrible job covering it up. There was no doubt in my mind that James was behind it. And despite what I knew he had done to her, I didn't even have to ask whose side she was on. I could sense it. She was with James.

"How could you betray me like that, Kate? My father loved you like his own child. Does that mean nothing to you? You're gonna throw it all away for some piece of shit that apparently beats you?"

"I don't have to answer to you, Amy." She answered with a scoff, acting surprised that I called her out on anything. "How I live my life is none of your business. I can tell you one thing, though. You and your boyfriend are both going to die today."

I was enraged. I couldn't control myself and I lunged for her. I grabbed her by the throat and pinned her to the ground. She gurgled as she struggled under my thumb. I couldn't believe the strength I had. I could see the hate and fear in her eyes… and it made me want to hurt her even smore.

My focus on Kate was so strong that I had tuned everything else out. I had completely lost track of Xavier and James. I was so entranced I don't think anything could have gotten my attention.

"This is for my dad!" I proclaimed loudly as I clamped down even harder. I broke her neck like it was nothing more than a pencil. A weak pencil at that. I stared down at her dead body in disbelief that I had just made that happen.

I turned to look behind me, but I was too late. I saw James on the same side of the riverbank running for Xavier. They would have been evenly matched if they had both been unarmed. I knew James would be carrying a weapon, though. He was too scared not to. I tried to run toward them, but I wasn't quick enough. James pulled out his gun and shot Xavier twice in the chest.

"James, you son of a bitch!" I yelled as tears began to stream down my face and Xavier fell to the ground. What had he done? Not now.

Without another word, my new instincts kicked in. I jumped high into the air and landed on James. I wanted to draw it out. I wanted to kill him slowly and make him beg for his life. He deserved it for what happened to dad, but I didn't have the time. I had to get Xavier home before he died too. So in one swift motion, I broke James's neck just like I did Kate's.

He was no match for my new power and speed. Now I could focus on somehow saving Xavier.

"Please hold on, I will have you home in a minute." I cried out to Xavier as I picked his bloody body off of the ground and began to run. Hopefully, no one would come though and see the bodies before I had a chance to get rid of them. Luckily, this was a part of the woods that people didn't typically frequent.

I ran as fast as I could back to Xavier's house. I wouldn't have made it there if I hadn't been immortal. It was so fast, I would be surprised if anyone even saw me. I kicked open his front door and put him on the couch. If only I knew the name of the doctor he called to help me. Then I wouldn't be on my own. My options were quickly running out. I got the immortality serum out of the safe, but by the time I made it back to him, he was unconscious.

I didn't know what to do. I know that the serum had to be injected, but how? There were so many ways to inject someone. Not to mention, he had to be close to death, but how close? I tried to take a deep breath and clear my mind. I checked his pulse and based on how shallow it was, I figured he was probably far enough gone for this to take. This would probably need to get into his bloodstream. The best way to get there would be to inject this into a vein. So I flipped over his arm and stabbed the syringe into the biggest vein I could see. I pushed the plunger down and began to cry. I wish I knew what I was doing.

I felt more alone now than when I first found out I was immortal. At least then I thought that Xavier wasn't going anywhere. Now he was on the brink of death and I didn't even know if I gave him the serum the right way. He said I was out for days, but I didn't know how long it took for the serum to wake me up.

The bullet wounds. He said that mine started disappearing. That would be a sure way to find out if the serum was working. I ripped off his shirt and grabbed the alcohol. I used it to rinse off the wounds. Once the blood was gone I would be able to see whether they were healing or not.

I sat there like an idiot just watching him, waiting for the wounds to heal. I kept taking his pulse to make sure that it wasn't getting worse. It was slow, but it was there. It wasn't getting any worse. At least he was alive.

Two hours had passed and there had been trivial improvement. I had been staring at his bullet wounds for so long, I couldn't tell if they were healing or if I was just imagining things. Silent tears were still streaming down my face. I felt so helpless. I didn't know what to do. I wish I knew more about that damn serum. I put my head in my hands and closed my eyes. I wished I could open them back up and realize that this had all been a bad dream. I knew that wouldn't happen so I kept them closed.

I knelt down on the floor next to the couch. I put my head on his chest. Please God, I didn't want to lose this man.

"Please, just wake up. I can't do this without you. I love you." I said out loud, still sobbing.

Then, Xavier took a deep breath, almost like a gasp. I picked my head up to look at him. His eyes weren't open and he still wasn't talking, but his wounds were beginning to heal. The holes were fading before my eyes. And just as they had disappeared completely, he opened his eyes.

"What happened? Why are you crying?" I wanted to laugh at his question. Based on how I felt, I was sure I looked like a total wreck. I had been going out of my mind this whole time and he didn't remember any of it.

"James shot you… twice in the chest. You lost a lot of blood and I thought you were going to die. I got a vial of serum out of the safe and injected you. I didn't think I did it right because nothing was happening, but your wounds started to heal and you woke up." I was ugly crying. I knew I couldn't hold it back, so I didn't even try.

Xavier just stared at me in wonder.

"So, I am immortal then?" He blinked slowly, taking everything I said in. I knew what his mind was going through. It was a lot to process.

"If I did it right, then yes. You must be, otherwise you would probably be dead right now. Unless I messed it up somehow and this is a false alarm. Is that possible? How do you feel? It was so bad. There was so much blood, Xavier." I was still sobbing and struggling to get my words out. I didn't know how much of it he was able to catch.

"I feel fine. I don't feel as if I have been shot." Xavier sat up and looked around. His whole house seemed to be covered in his blood. I was a mess myself. "But judging from all of this blood, you are telling me the truth. James and Kate are dead, right? I think I remember you killing them."

"Yeah, they are both dead. I can't believe they were still here. I thought for sure they would have been long gone. At least we don't have to worry about them anymore."

Xavier grabbed my hands and looked deep into my eyes.

"Thank you for saving me."

I just smiled at him and tried to wipe the tears that were still flowing off of my face.

"You up for a walk? We have a couple of bodies to hide if no one has come across them yet. If they have, I should probably go into hiding" I tried to laugh as if I were joking, but it was a legitimate concern for me right now. I wanted him to know what it was like now that he was immortal.

He nodded and got up. I shed my bloody clothes and grabbed some new ones from the stack that I kept here. I gave him some fresh clothes to throw on as well. I led him to the bathroom so we could quickly clean up a bit before we left. We couldn't just casually walk in the park covered in blood.

As we made our way out, I just watched him take everything in along the way. I think his scientific mind was trying to calculate the differences in everything he was doing.

"Is it all that you imagined?" I asked pulling him in close to me.

"All that and more. This is utterly amazing."

We made it to the river and to my relief, James and Kate were still there. Xavier pulled out his phone and made a call to someone. Their chat was brief. He told them to track his location and that there was a water balloon fight that needed to be cleaned up. After he hung up, he told me we could leave.

"A water balloon fight? Really?" I laughed and lightly slapped his arm.

"What? I could get on the phone and tell him to come dispose of a couple of bodies, Amy. Don't worry, it's someone we can trust. There is no need to worry. Let's go back to the park." He grabbed my hand and led me out of the woods.

EPILOGUE

We smiled as we held hands and walked down the pathway in the park. We took turns pointing things out to each other, such as flowers, birds, and random things that we had never noticed before. We stopped walking when we got to a bench and we took a seat.

"This has been one of the most interesting and amazing days of my life. If you would have told me a year ago that I would be sitting here with you today, both of us immortal and in love, I would have never believed it. You have transformed me from a lonely scientist into something on an entirely different level.

I could walk away from it all today and never look back as long as I have you with me."

I just smiled at him as I nuzzled my head into his shoulder.

"You saved me too babe. I can't imagine life without you. Just think, this is only the beginning."

We sat there for hours, just taking in everything. To think I passed out a few days ago and woke up this morning, immortal. I never knew where life would take me, but the universe sure did. I liked to think that my dad had a hand in it all too. After all, I was here with Xavier because of him.